SHOT TAKER

KING OF THE COURT #2

PIPER LAWSON

Content editing by Becca Mysoor
Line and copy editing by Cassie Robertson
Proofreading by Devon Burke
Cover design by Emily Wittig

For every girl
who longs for
a blank canvas

NOVA

"This gala is vital for the organization. You'll be creating the crown jewel of our facility."

The owner of the Kodiaks is shorter than the players but compensates for it with a suit and watch that look like they cost more than the trailer I grew up in.

"You'll have a budget for supplies and a stipend for living expenses. The balance will be transferred when the work is complete," he goes on.

"Thank you." I try to sound as serious as he looks, but secretly I'm buzzing with nervous excitement.

This is the opportunity of a lifetime.

Months ago, I was put on probation from my

job doing administration for a small design company.

Days ago, I was serving coffee a few blocks from my apartment in Boston.

Now...

I have the chance to show my work to millions of people.

The blank canvas could be the first thing that's truly mine. A bigger gift than the money or the exposure.

James Parker's office is dark wood and gold accents. You wouldn't know it had anything to do with basketball except for the awards in the case and the windows that overlook the court. It's clear he's into winning, or at least being seen as a winner.

He nods to a stack of papers between us, an NDA on top. "If you'll sign these."

I take a moment to scan the pages, skimming over the legal jargon. I don't want to miss anything important, but I'm also aware of him watching me.

Once I'm finished signing, I pass them back to him.

"You mentioned it's a mural for one of the central hallways in the arena. I've been working on some ideas." I pull out the sketches I drew on the plane from Boston yesterday. I'm glad I took an extra day to get here as I set the first concept in front of him. "I was thinking of the Kodiak logo, plus the players in action."

I flip to an outline of five guys around the basket, one going up for a dunk.

He glances at it before meeting my eyes again. "We need more."

"Thematically?"

"No, literally."

A ribbon of doubt cuts through my anticipation. "How big is the wall?"

He walks me down through the halls. With his lean figure and perfect posture, I'd bet he's closer to forty than fifty.

Staff nod to him, but in a deferential way rather than a friendly one.

It occurs to me he wasn't at the wedding.

Because he wasn't invited or because he declined to attend?

Maybe it was an impulsive idea to return to Denver...

For more reason than one.

He pulls up at the end of the hall that opens into a grand foyer and nods to the wall.

I stare down the length of it, my stomach dropping. "Holy. This entire thing?"

"The entire thing." He smiles. "You have three months."

I've only ever done small drawings and paintings, nothing of this scale. Brooke was right when she said James Parker didn't do things halfway.

"Why me?"

The owner folds his arms, the diamond face of his watch glinting in the light. "Because timing is everything. And right now, you're who everyone wants."

Not everyone.

My mind flashes to Clay.

The Kodiaks' all-star power forward.

The gorgeous, rich athlete who dragged me into his world, who kissed me like he needed me and told me without words that I belonged here.

When the offer from the Kodiaks' owner came in, coming back and confronting all those emotions I tried to leave behind seemed insane.

But I have friends here.

Family.

I loved the time I spent in Denver leading up to the wedding. Except...

The hairs on my neck lift. I turn, half expecting to find Clay standing there. He's not, but there's a full-story image of Clay on the opposite wall. He's dressed in his Kodiaks uniform, palming a ball with one hand and eyeing the camera as though he's a bear that could swipe it to the ground if it looks at him wrong.

Since the Kodiaks Camp charity auction, my online following has been doubling every week. But with the *Architectural Digest* feature, it exploded.

People I barely know have reached out to congratulate me, but I've heard silence from the man who broke my heart with a letter.

Clay said he didn't want me.

That we were nothing.

He hurt me in the worst possible way.

After my fiancé left with zero notice, all of our money, and a bunch of revenue from client projects at the design firm, I trusted Clay and believed he was different. I was different with him.

Until it was over.

We might not be on speaking terms, but he'll be watching me work.

"Access has been restricted to this area, so only staff and players can go here. You won't be interrupted, even when the public is in the building."

The owner misreads my concern.

"I have headphones." I gesture to my bag. "No one will bother me."

A custodian arrives, driving a small cart. The owner waits for him to remove a ladder from the back and set it up for me.

"You best get started."

"Thank you, Mr. Parker."

He surveys me from the tips of my shoes to my pink hair. "Call me James."

He pivots on one expensive dress shoe, and I turn back to the wall.

It's fifty feet long and one and a half stories high. A huge mural on display for the team, the city, the world.

I checked the schedule before I came over to the stadium today. The team is on back-to-backs, which means no practice. They'll be rehabbing and arrive just in time for shootaround and the game.

Today, this echoing place is mine.

CLAY

"Second day of a back-to-back. How do you feel about your chances?" the reporter asks eagerly at our pregame press conference.

"Same as I feel every night—like we'll win."

At this point in the season, there's a routine to giving comments. They're the right words on an endless loop.

"Do you think the Kodiaks will make it into the playoffs this year? And if not, what does that mean for you?"

"We're here to go as deep as we can."

"Trade talks have been swirling," begins another reporter, "and your name has been mentioned."

The room goes quiet.

I shift in my seat, and every eye in the room follows the movement. They're reading into each blink and breath and cough.

Chloe's at my side, her knuckles cracking against her iPad.

"I'm here to play ball," I say evenly. "The rest is above my paygrade."

Chloe nods, which means I'm off the hook. I shift out of the chair and shoulder my gym bag, putting on my Beats headphones as I leave to prep for the game.

The past few weeks have been a blur. Work out, play, get on a plane, repeat. The schedule never bothered me before, but now I'm finding fault with what used to be my comfort.

Probably because of the throbbing ache in my gut and chest that never goes away.

Sometimes when I'm giving it everything, I swear it'll be enough to take the edge off. If I'm tired enough, I won't have the energy to feel this.

It's getting better.

That's what I tell myself.

Like rehabbing an injury, you have to believe it's one percent improved every time you go through the routine. In sports and in life, momentum is everything.

Over enough time, one percent adds up.

The halls are nearly empty. No one knows about my deal with Harlan or that I'm still waiting on a trade to LA. It's getting more frustrating by the day to put in my max effort here when I know I won't be in Denver through the end of the season.

Not that I've been an antisocial prick the past month.

I've helped Rookie with his jump shot.

Went sneaker shopping with Jay.

Hell, I even dog-sat Waffles one afternoon for Miles.

What I'm not doing is answering any of the women who've hit me up.

None of them have pink hair and slow curves and a smile that makes the world brighten like a rainbow after a storm.

Thinking of the woman who came into my life out of nowhere and blew out of it just as fast makes my chest ache.

But I ended it because she's better off being halfway across the country living her safe life without me.

I tell myself that late at night when I'm restless

in an unfamiliar bed and so starved for a taste of her that I'd settle for listening to her voicemail greeting on repeat just to feel like we're still talking.

With ninety minutes to the game, I need to start my routine. Then shootaround and tip-off, then I can take an ice bath, crawl into bed, and sleep for ten hours.

I don't want to see anyone from the team, so I take the longer, more public route to get to the home locker room.

The music pulses in my ears, vibrating through my muscles, joints, skin.

When I head into one of the open hallways, every part of me stiffens. I pull up, and my bag thuds against the floor.

Her back is to me, the back pockets of her tight jeans at eye level as she stands on the ladder, her weight on one hip. Her hair tumbles down her shoulders, headphones tucked between the hot pink strands.

She's here.

Nova's at my workplace, in my jungle, taking up space like a pink neon sign declaring, "In your dreams."

The feeling in my gut isn't sadness but longing.

A throbbing ache that swells until it consumes all of me.

I'm not over her.

Not one percent, not anything.

Forcing my feet to move, I grab my bag and change directions.

"What the fuck are you playing at?" I slam the door of Harlan's office behind me.

Harlan looks up, surprised. "You have a game."

"The game can wait for an explanation."

"I have no idea what you're talking about."

I drop the bag and pace the room. "Don't lie to me. We made a deal. You'd get me LA if I stayed away. How the hell am I supposed to do that when she's parked in my commute?"

"Who?"

"Nova." Saying her name hurts. The ache in my chest takes root, deepening and spreading to my lungs, my gut.

Harlan's expression sharpens. "Impossible. She went back to Boston."

I stab a finger at the door. "She's on a ladder in

the lobby, staring at a wall like it's playing HB-fucking-O."

He frowns, his gaze dropping to the desk.

"You didn't know," I realize.

"The tenth-anniversary gala in February. James wants to make it a showcase, a triumph. Celebrities, music, art."

The owner is a spoiled rich asshole who cares more about style than substance, but I'm not sure what he has to do with...

Art.

A piece clicks into place.

"He wants her to paint the wall."

"What wall?" Harlan asks.

"The big fucking blank wall in the foyer."

Harlan sighs.

"I'll talk to him. If he hasn't made a contract, there could be time to get rid of her. Assuming that's what you want." He shifts back, and I'm already seeing where he's going. "It would be a big break for her. Her drawings at the auction were one thing, but art commissioned for the team? That gets seen by millions of people. It could make her career."

Damn it.

I know how important getting your big break is.

She's talented and hardworking, and she deserves it. Everything she's done is to be independent and stand on her own feet.

And if I end this, I'll be the prick who took that from her.

"Our deal stands," he reminds me. "Nothing has to change."

The deal where he gets me my trade to LA, all but guaranteeing me the golden legacy I've spent my entire career chasing, and all I have to do is stay away from her.

"Yeah, and how's that deal coming?" I demand, needing somewhere to focus that's not the girl living rent free in my head.

"A few more weeks."

I stare at the photos on his wall. Teams Harlan's worked with over the years.

He wants a win here. He and I disagree on a lot of things, but he won't compromise that goal.

Nova returning wasn't Harlan's doing. He might fuck with people, but he's not willing to risk the team's future for this.

No, this is the owner imposing his frivolous will and not having a clue what he's getting into.

Which in some ways makes this worse, because I have no one to take it out on.

My phone rings.

Coach.

I hit Accept.

"WADE!!! I don't care how much your ass is worth—"

"Be there in five," I answer, clicking off.

I shove the phone in my track pants and reach for my headphones. "She should work when the team isn't here. She'll be in the way."

I start for the door, reaching it before I hear Harlan's chair scrape the floor as he rises.

"You really cared about her, didn't you?" he asks, his voice lower than before.

I slip my headphones over my ears and pretend I don't hear him.

3

NOVA

*O*nce I started staring at the wall, the music in my headphones grabbed me. It took an hour to ignore Clay's eyes at my back, but now I barely feel them as the mural takes shape in my mind.

It's about the blue. The clouds, the atmosphere, all of it blending with the mountains guarding the skyline.

After my conversation with James, I was intimidated by the need to create way more than I'd planned. But I've drawn it in my sketchpad, made some changes. I erased the parts I got wrong.

It's easy to get swept up in the simple joy of creating. I've been standing like this, leaning over the seat of the ladder, for so long my foot is numb. When I stand and stretch, my muscles spasm.

I hear what sounds like my name, but it's far away. When I twist toward the sound, Miles is coming down the hallway, Jayden at his side. His expression is bright with happiness and surprise.

I catch a toe and slip.

The floor hurtles upward, my sketchpad flies through the air.

"Nova!"

"Shit," comes another voice. Jayden's maybe.

I was always so worried about dying in a plane that I never stopped to think about the more boring ways I might go.

But now, I'm going to land on my head in the middle of the Kodiaks' arena.

This is it...

I squeeze my eyes shut.

My head hits a hard chest, and muscled limbs band around my ribs and legs.

It's more welcoming than the floor.

Barely, I decide as I look up into Clay's face.

He's more gorgeous than I remember.

His hair curls around his ears, brushing his neck. His brows are pulled into a line. He's clean shaven for once, which only makes his firm mouth stand out.

But it's his eyes, dark and full of concern, that trap me.

Clay's skin brands my exposed legs, our breath mingling.

He doesn't say anything, but I swear the air between us throbs.

A dozen memories race up at me, like the floor was racing up at me a moment ago.

My heart feels as if it's going to beat out of my chest, pounding against his.

Someone clears their throat, and Clay practically drops me on my feet.

"Damn, that was close. You okay?" Miles asks.

"You shouldn't yell at girls on ladders, dumbass," Jayden chides.

"I'm fine," I murmur as I turn, reaching for my sketchpad on the floor.

"She was obviously lining up to fall into my arms," Miles goes on. "Clay had better timing for once."

"I have better timing always." The low, familiar voice has the hairs on my arms lifting.

When I straighten, I rub my arms where he touched me. I half expect Clay to tell Miles to back the hell off because he's always been possessive, but Clay's the one who steps back.

"Thought you went back to... Boston, right?" Jay asks.

I nod. "James called with an offer I couldn't refuse."

Clay's eyes bore into me, but I focus on Miles.

"So, you're back!" Miles is enthusiastic. "How long are you staying?"

Clay pulls out his phone and starts typing.

"Ah. Until I finish this mural for the Kodiaks' anniversary gala."

I pretend I don't care if he's talking to a woman. So what if one of the Kodashians is keeping his bed warm?

I was never in it.

A spot on my arm where he caught me burns, and I rub it absently. Clay's gaze lifts from his phone to follow the motion.

Even when he's not trying to leave a mark, he manages to.

"What a little gathering."

The familiar voice and sound of shoes down the hall has us all turning to see Harlan, his smile wide.

Clay, already at arm's length, steps back further.

Can he really not stand the sight of me?

"Hello, Nova." Harlan smiles. "Welcome back."

"Hi." I force a smile in return.

"Gentlemen, there's a team meeting before you all go home. Coach promised to keep it short."

The guys grumble about their plans and the rest they'd been hoping to get as they follow Harlan down the hall.

All except Clay.

He's rooted to the ground, his eyes changing color from caramel to chocolate.

His gaze falls to my arm again, the red mark where he caught me standing out against my pale skin.

Clay frowns. "I didn't mean to hurt you."

My chest knots. He hurt me so much worse a month ago.

"I can take it." I drag the headphones off my neck and wind the cord in my hands. "I should get back to work, and it sounds like you should too."

I arch a brow, hoping I look bored rather than unnerved.

Clay bends to pick up my fallen pencils one by

one. He straightens and places them in my hand, folding my fingers closed around them.

"I like your hair."

My breath catches, and I resist the urge to play with the strands I had a few inches chopped off before coming here as he turns to follow the others down the hall.

The lobby is full of suits and skirts. I scan the crowd before landing on Mari getting out of an elevator at her office building.

My sister's green jacket looks amazing with her dark hair, a chic bob. She spots me a moment after I see her, and we meet in the middle.

"Meeting ran late," Mari says, wrapping me in a hug.

"It's okay. Want to grab a drink?"

We head toward the front doors and out onto the street.

I'd finally started to shake off the feeling of my run in with Clay, reminding myself that thousands of people work in this city without sparing a thought for the grumpy power forward, when Mari texted to demand how long I've been in town and when I had been planning to tell her.

"Harlan said you're doing art for the team?" she asks as we take a right down the bustling sidewalk.

"The owner invited me. It was a surprise to say the least."

"It's weird."

I cut her a look. "One of the drawings I did for the auction wound up in *Architectural Digest*."

"How did that happen?"

"I have no idea," I admit.

She frowns. "I'm not saying you're not great, but... James and Harlan have a rough relationship."

"The guy hired him. How rough can it be?"

We get to the cocktail bar and find our way to a high top table. Once we're settled, we order a wine for Mari and a G&T for me.

"How is married life?" I ask.

"Harlan's amazing. The honeymoon was everything I imagined." Her face transforms into a smile. "He does the sweetest things for me. Rubs my feet when I'm stressed from work. Tells me I'm the best."

My chest aches a little. "And what do you do for him?"

She turns it over. "I listen. He has exacting standards for himself, but he's better at managing it than I am. There's a lot going on with the team."

I want to press her for details but remind myself it's not my problem.

So, we catch up over our drinks, talking about work and life and friends. Since the wedding, it's felt as if we're on more even ground for once.

"It's Chloe's birthday this week," she says before finishing her wine. "A bunch of us girls are going to the pub. You should come."

I like that Mari's making an effort to include me. "Sure. I'm in." My phone buzzes, so I check it. "I need to go meet Brooke. She said I could stay with her for now."

"You can stay with us, you know. We'd barely notice you in the house."

"Thanks, but I'm trying to spread my freeloading around."

Mari laughs. "Do you need a ride?"

"It's not far, and Brooke already took my bag from the airport."

I hug my sister, and we go our separate ways.

As I make the walk to Brooke's condo building, I'm thinking of how good things are with Mari compared to when I came for the first time. It's for the best that my relationship with Clay, if you can even call it that, didn't come out before the wedding.

Now, there's nothing to come out. He made it clear we might as well be strangers.

After weeks of cradling my broken heart, maybe it's better this way.

I'll see him at the arena and barely even then. If he wants to be weird if we pass in the hallway, that's on him.

And I can always flip off Wall Clay if I need to vent.

There's no reason to spend more time with the real thing.

On my way, I stop at a bakery to grab some donuts for my friend.

Reemerging with a half dozen treats tucked under my arm, I check the address Brooke gave me. It feels familiar, but I can't put my finger on why.

When I pull up at the doors, my stomach sinks.

I look up at the condo building looming overhead.

The condo building I've definitely been to once before.

Clay's building.

~

"Hi, friend!" Brooke squeals as the door swings open. "I'm so glad you could stay with me. Between us, I've been needing some girl time. Oh my God, are those donuts?!"

Her enthusiasm deflates my idea to text Mari and see if she's still open to a houseguest until I have enough for rent on my own.

Brooke takes me on a tour. The kitchen is beautiful. The apartment is like Clay's, but it has different finishes. More feminine furniture and paint colors.

"Do a lot of team people live in this building?"

"A few." Realization settles on her face. "Oh, you mean because Clay does."

"You could've told me." But the moment it's out, I feel like a jerk. She's doing me a huge favor.

"He's on a different floor."

Maybe she's right. The man caught me when I fell off a ladder and couldn't wait to get away from me. At this point, he'd probably wait for another elevator just to avoid me.

Brooke sinks onto the couch in an elegant move, depositing the box of treats on the coffee table and motioning me to join her. "You never told me what happened the night of the wedding. Not the details, anyway."

"He left me a letter saying we were nothing. Basically, the same as my ex when he disappeared. At least Clay had it hand-delivered."

Her expression darkens. "That's really shitty. I'm sorry."

"He never promised anything. And I should have known better than to think he cared about me." After what Brad did, I should have seen it coming.

She makes a sound of understanding. "Guys aren't worth the hassle. I'm going to make this better for you. You'll forget all about him."

Brooke rises and holds out a hand. I take it and follow her to the bedrooms.

"This is you."

I gasp as I look around the huge room, my suitcase already laid on a luggage rack. "It's beautiful. This bed..."

"I figured you'd like pink." She grins. "This is your closet." She throws open the doors and steps inside.

"You could have a party in there."

"You will. But while we're on the topic, you

don't have enough clothes to fill this. We need to go shopping tomorrow."

I open my mouth to protest but stop. "I have a stipend for my job, but I want to cover my half of rent."

She waves. "The place is paid up for the year. And you brought donuts."

I blink at her. The donuts weren't cheap, but they were significantly less than housing.

"You can pay for internet if you're desperate to feel like you're contributing," she goes on at my look.

"Brooke, you're unreal." I'm embarrassed to feel tears sting the backs of my eyes.

"We're going to have the best time. Two single girls conquering the city. They'll make an adaptation of our exploits."

I laugh, getting swept up in her enthusiasm. "Like *Girls* or *Sex and the City*?"

"More like *Troy*."

4

CLAY

"*I* said no gifts," Chloe chides as the presents pile up on the table at Mile High.

"Yeah, but you didn't mean it," Jay says.

Chloe swats at him, and he grins.

Birthdays aren't worth celebrating, at least when they're mine. Another year around the sun with my body reminding me I'm not what I used to be.

But today isn't *my* birthday, so the celebration is easier.

This week, I could use the distraction from the messy feelings that have been following me everywhere since I learned Nova was back.

The distance from here to Boston wasn't enough to keep me from thinking of her.

Having her occupy the same city is fucking with my head.

Chloe said she was going out with friends tonight, but Miles and I are friendly, and Jay's in that friend/ex-boyfriend zone, so by that point, the entire team was coming. So, we ambushed her at the pub.

"What the hell? I thought we were early!" Brooke walks in.

"You are early. I was abducted by a bunch of players," Chloe says.

"Don't pretend this isn't your fantasy every night," Miles says.

She tosses him a look. "If I'm going to be at the center of a harem, I'd prefer hockey players."

Jay shudders. "They smell, Chlo."

"Weird superstitions," Miles adds.

"No teeth," I volunteer.

She laughs, but my chest tightens when I see Mari and Nova come in the door behind Brooke.

Nova's wearing leggings, black boots, and a sweater under her jacket. She's laughing until she sees me and her smile fades.

It's hard enough pretending to the world that I don't care about her.

Making her believe it is another level of torture.

The booth seats eight comfortably, and there are six of us—but five are massive.

On my side, Atlas is on the inside, Miles in the middle, and me outside.

Opposite us, Mari shifts in next to Rookie, squeezing Chloe tighter between him and Jay.

"Nova, sit here. I'll get a chair." Miles climbs over me, leaving an empty spot in the middle of the bench.

"What am I?" Brooke demands as Miles grabs one chair, then a second.

"My lady." He holds one out while Brooke sinks into the seat.

Nova's eyes lock with mine.

I'm used to keeping my feelings inside, but now I have to look her in the eye and act like she's not the one I think about every night.

She doesn't want to sit next to me, but avoiding it is more awkward.

I move over without a word and Nova drops onto the booth next to me, leaving as much space between us as possible without her falling out of the booth.

So, basically an inch.

Her light floral scent invades my nostrils, like it did the other day when she slipped right off that ladder and scared the shit out of me.

Catching her in my arms might have saved her pink head, but it fucked with mine.

I'll get through the next hour without breathing. No problem.

"Can I get you a drink?" Miles asks Nova.

"Sure, thanks."

Miles takes off to the bar faster than I've ever seen him get back on defense on the court.

"I'll have a Coke," Brooke calls after him.

Jay produces a small box and holds it out. "Happy birthday, Chloe."

She looks at him in surprise. "You shouldn't have."

She unwraps it, and it's an expensive watch.

"It's beautiful, Jay."

Miles returns with drinks, sliding Nova's and Brooke's over to them.

Nova smiles at him, and I grind my molars.

"Here's one from me." Rookie slides over a small wrapped rectangle.

Chloe tugs at the paper to reveal a book. "*The Seven Husbands of Evelyn Hugo*. And it's signed?"

she goes on as she opens the cover, her lips parting in delight.

Jayden's eyes narrow.

"She posted a Taylor Jenkins Reid book on her socials a while back. I pay attention," Rookie says.

"You pay attention like that on the court, you'd be making ten assists a game," Jay says.

"Come on, that's your job." Rookie grins.

Jay doesn't look happy the twenty-year-old is flirting with his ex. Can't say I blame him.

Brooke passes a wrapped box to Chloe. "This is from me. And Nova. Since we're roommates, we do joint gifts."

"You're what?" I grunt.

"Nova's staying with me," Brooke says breezily.

My hands fist under the table.

Because it wasn't brutal enough already that she's under the same roof as me during the day, now I know she's there at night too.

Chloe opens the gift and raises her brows as she takes in the small purple object about the size of her palm. "It's a vibrator."

"The best vibrator," Brooke explains as though she hands out sex toys every day of the week. "Different speeds, vibration patterns—pretty cool stuff. It even has an app so you can control it remotely—which makes long distance relationships a lot easier."

Miles frowns. "But it's not—"

"A cock? The best things aren't."

"Is that true?" Miles asks Nova with a grin.

Nova laughs. "Women are better at getting themselves off than guys are at getting them off."

I take a sip of my drink like I'm not remembering how she looked touching herself in the bunkbeds at Kodiak Camp, her skin shining with lake water and sweat.

Brooke nods. "Toys can be a great way to explore different sensations and figure out what works for you. You can find lots of ways to use it with a partner or even solo!"

"When's your birthday, Nova?" Miles asks.

"In the spring."

"You want a vibrator or a watch or a book? I'm taking notes." He grins.

"If I wanted a vibrator, I'd go out and get one. Spring's a long time to go without satisfaction."

The group erupts. Jay cracks up, and Brooke claps her hands in delight.

What the fuck?

Nova's holding court in the middle of the team —*my* team—like it's hers and I don't even exist.

Miles leans in. "If I can help in that department..."

She smiles into her drink. "I have your number."

I've always thought the league needed more quality shooting guards.

Shame we're going to be down one when Miles meets his demise in about five goddamn seconds.

I have zero problem with a woman taking things into her own hands. It's healthy and sexy, and watching Nova do just that gave me enough material to last until all-star break.

But if those hands are anyone else's...

"I mean it. You want to experiment, I'm your guy," Miles goes on, oblivious.

My brain is a second from imploding, and I swear I hear the clock ticking down.

"You're not her type," Mari says to Miles. "Nova likes good boys."

I cough.

"My sister's right," Nova says, her gaze flicking to me as she shifts in her seat. "I like men who are emotionally available. And who have space next to their overinflated egos."

Hollers go up.

Bullshit.

It's one thing for her to think I ended it, that I don't care, as long as it gets her living her best life.

Watching her laugh with my friends, get hit on by my teammate, act like she and I never had *anything*, is not in the cards.

I'm tense as I lean forward to rest my elbows on the table, knocking a butter knife off into Nova's lap the process.

"Sorry," I mutter.

I reach for it, but she's faster, scooting closer to me and retrieving from her other side.

My hand lands on her thigh.

Nova inhales sharply.

"A guy without an ego isn't good enough at his job," Miles says, oblivious.

"What if he's just humble?" Chloe contends.

Jay smirks. "In sex or basketball, there's no such thing."

The group continues talking, but I'm focused on her.

Her softness. Her warmth through the leggings.

I should pull back, but I don't.

I've gone weeks without touching her and I can't bring myself to stop.

Nova grips the knife in one hand and reaches

for her drink with the other, her knuckles going white as she takes a long sip.

"Come on, Clay, back me up," Jay chides.

I lean my free arm along the back of the booth. "Sounds like you're doing just fine."

My hand inches higher.

Nova's thighs squeeze together, trapping my fingers.

"It's not ego because before you get there, it's your responsibility to make sure you are the best," Miles jumps in.

Another inch.

She bites her lip, shifting in her seat.

They're all engaged in this topic, but I'm thinking only of her.

"That's it," Jay agrees. "You gotta hold up your head and know that you're taking care of business. *All* your business."

Now, I'm touching her through two layers of fabric instead of one.

Nova's breath catches, and she makes a strangled sound.

Fuck, she's hot.

And wet.

My knuckle rubs back and forth.

Her eyes meet mine, full of arousal and anger in equal measure.

Nova shoves my hand away and takes off toward the back of the bar, leaving us staring after her.

"She had three cappuccinos today," Brooke supplies, and the others shrug it off.

I wait two minutes before I go after her, pacing the hallway between the bathrooms.

Feeling her up in a moment of insanity at a public bar? Not my finest move.

But I was coming out of my skin. I could never keep my head on straight around her, and I guess some things haven't changed.

I'm planning to apologize, but when Nova comes out of the bathroom, she grabs my wrist and drags me into a pitch-black storage room.

"What the hell was that?" she demands in the dark.

"Dropped a knife."

"It didn't fall into my underwear."

My chest heaves. "You and Miles were one mixed drink away from getting a room."

"I don't see how it's any of your business."

"It is when you're wet for me." I reach for the light switch and slam it on. "You once told me how much these fingers turned you on," I continue, lifting my hand. "You can taste them again if you doubt your memory."

Her eyes widen with blue fire, her pink hair swinging around her shoulders. "My body doesn't call the shots anymore, and I don't owe anything to a man who ended things in a letter the same way my ex did."

She hurls the words at me like attack, but she's the one who looks wounded. It's not the accusation on her face but the hurt beneath that guts me.

I wanted to make room for her to choose for herself, to know she was enough. Instead, I gave her another reason to believe she wasn't.

How fucking callous I must have seemed.

"You didn't want me then. I'm not yours now," she goes on, her voice wavering at the edges. "If you need that hand to play basketball, you'll think twice before touching me with it again."

She spins and heads back out, letting the door slam behind her.

5

CLAY

"Utah are grinders on defense." Coach points at the screen in the dark theater room. "Watch these rotations."

We're reviewing game tape in our team meeting, and I shift back, extending my legs over the seat in front of me. Utah is technically sound but not as physical as LA.

Which is why instead of going over matchups, my mind cuts to wondering if a certain pink-haired princess is occupying a hallway a few hundred feet from here.

Now that I know how bad I hurt her, I can't think of anything else.

She's under my skin, in my blood, on my brain.

I've built an exceptional career being a selfish prick, but where she's concerned...

I hate living in a world where she thinks I'm an asshole.

I don't live my life regretting where I've been, but I can't help wondering if I made the wrong call with her.

With us.

"... we're going to make the playoffs, we gotta take Utah for three of four."

The playoffs. I'm trying not to think that far ahead because if everything goes to plan, I won't be in a Kodiaks uniform, but the excited rumble through the room makes it impossible to ignore.

Harlan promised to get me out, but for the time being, I'm still here, surrounded by guys who want to win in this city—for this city.

A hand goes up. *Rookie*. "We can get through them. They'll be playing catch-up the entire night."

Miles hollers and fist-bumps Rookie.

"Wade," Coach barks, and all heads turn toward me. "You've played Utah plenty. Got any input?"

"I can get past their guards. Center's a step slow."

"What about for the rest of the team?"

I pause. "That's above my paygrade."

Later, on my way out of the room, Coach grabs me. "I need you to step up. You're used to seeing the game for you, but the next evolution is you seeing it for all of them."

I cock my head. "Next evolution of my game is holding the MVP trophy at finals."

He swears. "You don't get there without four other guys. This game isn't only about stars, Wade. Someone has to take responsibility for this team."

"That's your job, old man."

"What about when I'm gone?"

I scoff. "You're gonna outlive us all in this league."

After banging out the routine, my muscles are straining and my lungs burning. I grab a towel and wipe down, watching Rookie do lunges across the gym.

I'm never gonna be the leader Coach wants. I'm too focused on my own game.

But in the young guy working his ass off on the other side of the floor, I see a piece of myself.

"Your handle's not gonna work against him," I tell Rookie gruffly, naming one of the guards on the opposing team. "He'll pick your pocket all night long. Best you can do is try to switch onto the four or five."

His brows rise, his breath straining as he repeats the movement. "You don't think I can take him?"

Doesn't matter what I think, what matters is what Rookie thinks. What he's committed to doing.

And there's uncertainty in his eyes.

I might not know how to fix things with Nova, but this, I can fix.

"I bet you five large you can't take him," I say.

Rookie grins against the effort. "I'll prove it to you."

NOVA

There is no better companion for painting than Lizzo. She's the best friend you never knew you needed cheering you on.

While she's been blasting from my headphones, I've painted the skyline twice. It's the part of the wall that will be the grandest but also the most straightforward. The individual components are inanimate—buildings don't have souls until they're filled with people—while the other pieces of the mural will be more challenging to get right. It's not enough that the brushstrokes are accurate. They have to feel alive.

Bumping into Clay at Chloe's party had my emotions running high.

I still get hot thinking about how he slipped his huge hand over my thigh as if my body was his to command.

Hot with anger. Not arousal.

I swore I wouldn't get off to him. It was part of the deal I made myself when I lit his jersey on fire.

No more fantasizing about Clayton Wade.

I didn't plan on telling him how much he'd hurt me, but there was a flicker of shock and regret on his face when I did.

Well, I'm over it. Clay's used to getting what he wants when he wants it and casting it aside just as fast.

In the past week, I've been here early every morning working on the skyline that will form the foundation of the first part of the mural. It feels good to be making progress.

I tug the headphones off and step down for a break when I hear my name.

"Nova."

I spin, wiping at my brow. "Hi, Mr. Parker."

"James," he says. "How is my wall? I need a photo to show stakeholders."

"Soon," I say.

James glances at his watch before meeting my eyes again with a smile. "By five?"

My stomach lurches as I realize how quickly I'll have to finish in order for it to be presentable for a photo.

His tone implies that if it's not done by then, there will be consequences for me personally. I read the paperwork as thoroughly as I could, but who knows if he could withhold my paycheck or maybe even fire me and start over with another artist?

"Of course," I say, trying to sound confident.

My mind spins as I try to calculate how much more time it will take me to finish up this one area of the mural while being careful not to mess with anything else.

My back is already sore from bending and stretching, and I rub my hip absently as I survey what still needs to be done.

Three hours later, I'm still stretched out, my muscles complaining. I haven't stopped for a bathroom break or anything else in as long as I can remember.

Why the hell did I promise to get this done today?

There's one spot that's high enough I might need a new ladder, but facilities hasn't responded to my call and I don't have time to go hunting for them.

My headphone batteries die, and I toss them onto my bag at the foot of the ladder. Even Lizzo has quit for the day.

I bend my forehead against the ladder and press my palm to my face.

"*The Thinker*. It's a famous statue."

Clay's voice has me dragging a raw breath through my lungs.

He's obviously finished practice, wearing a camel Vuitton sweater and jeans. The dark lines trailing out from under the pushed-up sleeves make my thighs clench.

"Didn't peg you as a Rodin fan."

"I've seen most of his works, but I prefer *The Kiss*."

I look up at him, wary. "Because it's romantic?"

"Because it's tragic. A noblewoman who fell in love with her husband's younger brother. In

Dante's *Inferno*, they were condemned to wander hell for their sins."

Okay, I'm not at all interested in Clay's knowledge of art.

I try once more to stretch and reach, but I can't. I screech in frustration and drop back to my heels.

"What's wrong?"

"With us?" I'm incredulous.

"No, I mean right now."

I want to tell him to get out of here, but I'm intimidated by the owner's demand and frazzled about how best to comply.

I nod toward the wall. "James wants this done today so he can show some board members the progress. I need to finish that part." I point toward the top corner. "And I already chipped two nails trying, which sucks because Brooke and I only got them done yesterday."

I hold out my hand as if the broken nails are proof of something broken in me.

Clay looks between me and the wall. "Come here."

I stiffen.

"If you don't get down from there"—he nods toward the ladder—"I can't get up."

What?

He means...

Oh.

"You can't," I say plainly. "You don't have the right technique."

"I'm good with my hands."

Now, I'm remembering the feel of him touching me. What would have happened if I hadn't gotten up and run out?

I shove the thoughts down.

"You don't listen," I contend. "You do things your own way, and if you don't do them my way, you'll ruin it."

"It's sky. How bad can I fuck that up? And if I do, you paint over it."

Okay, technically he's not wrong.

I cut him a look. "I'm surprised you're admitting it's possible for you to fuck up."

A muscle in his jaw twitches. "I fuck up plenty, Nova."

It's not an apology, but there's a hint of humility in the words.

Clay gaze lowers to the airbrush in my hands. "We'll do this your way. Talk me through it."

I don't want him to be part of my art, forever part of this installation that's mine.

But the other option is not completing this milestone for the owner.

So, I step down carefully, moving to the side and holding out the airbrush. Our fingers brush as he takes it. Clay takes three steps up the ladder, then another two without pausing. He's already taller than I was.

"Your knee—" I start.

"I can play basketball, I can stand on a ladder."

He leans toward the corner in question, and my heart leaps into my throat. This was a bad idea. He could still ruin this. Or fall and hurt himself and be useless to the team.

I should find facilities and get their help.

But he's already sizing up the area to paint.

"Go slow," I say. "Don't press, squeeze lightly. The color looks like it's not coming out at first, but it is."

Clay's face scrunches up in concentration, the same way as when he's analyzing a defense to break down.

The blue mists onto the wall, and my breath catches.

"Move around," I say quickly. I should have led with that. "Smooth strokes, nothing jerky."

He does what I say, and the rich color floods the wall. I keep guiding him with my voice.

"That's not bad," I admit.

His mouth curves at the corner. "You like telling me what to do."

"Only when you listen."

The low sound from his throat could be a muffled chuckle, and damn if it doesn't make my chest ache.

It's not as if he cares about me.

He went out of his way to make sure I knew that.

Maybe he didn't realize how much he hurt me when he broke things off, and now he feels guilty about it.

But as I watch him work, the deliberateness of every stroke, it softens me.

I'm remembering how good it felt to be with him. How I swore I saw him and he saw me. He's the first person who really believed in me as an artist.

"Stop," I bark after ten or fifteen minutes of me directing him.

He looks down, quizzical.

I survey the wall in its entirety. "I think that's it."

Clay steps down and holds out the airbrush.

We're standing too close, and I take a stiff step back. "Could you move the ladder?"

He carries it easily a dozen steps away before returning.

I'm scanning the wall with a critical eye when I glance over and spot droplets of blue on his expensive sweater.

My stomach sinks.

I grab his arm without thinking, tugging at the fabric to see if the stain was a trick of the light.

No luck. There's an aqua mist drying on half his forearm.

"Oh no..."

One time, Brad's white shirt got a paint stain on it. He was annoyed for weeks, and it probably cost a fraction of what Clay's wearing.

"Hey." He lifts my chin with his finger and forces me to look up at the straight nose, dark eyes, and firm lips I've traced so often in my dreams. "I don't give a shit about the sweater."

Suddenly, I'm thinking of how we laughed at Red Rocks, running across the landscape. The night he held me at his place after the ruined bachelorette party—

My attention jerks back to the wall.

I lift my phone and adjust the filters so the light bathes every inch of the buildings, sky, clouds, and birds.

I snap a picture, inspecting the image with the same intensity.

Is that part of the sky uneven, or is it just the light?

I lift my finger to point at the wall. "Right there. I should probably fix..."

"Nova." He grabs my hand out of the air, squeezing it in his. "It's beautiful."

My stomach flutters. In the moment before I pull away, his fingers feel like a lot of things.

Guilt isn't one of them.

6

CLAY

The Utah game starts with a bang.

The crowd is into it from tip-off.

Atlas knocks the ball to Jay, who brings it up the court and finds me early.

They're guarding me close, so I sidestep to shake them and sink a three over the startled second-year guard's head.

"Fuck yeah!" Rookie grins at me, and I grin back.

That's how it goes.

Back and forth, fast-paced with lots of buckets. Everyone's getting theirs tonight, Jay and Miles and even Atlas down low.

I've got energy to burn tonight, and it feels good to put it all out there on the court.

Partway through the first quarter, I pass to a cutting Rookie even though I have a clear shot. He dunks it over one defender, and satisfaction slams into me.

I look up, half expecting to see Nova watching, but she's not there. It's only James Parker in the box, looking right at me.

Since I signed here, Harlan and I have had our problems, but the Kodiaks owner is a whole other issue.

He has a reputation for wanting control, and for collecting pretty things: houses, boats, a couple of islands. His money came from family and finance, and everyone was surprised when he bought the franchise because no one knew he was even a basketball fan.

But so far, he's been willing to fund the budget for a growing team, so people keep quiet about the rest.

I don't like that he approached Nova. I don't want him thinking he can collect her.

End of the first half, we're fist-bumping on the way to the locker room.

"That was impressive. If you were watching the offensive end," Coach says to me.

"Coach, we're up by twelve."

"We could be up by twenty-five if you played defense."

I drop a towel over my head and breathe in. Adrenaline pumps in my veins as my body recovers from the effort.

Suddenly, I'm not thinking of the game but of Nova. Yesterday, I wanted to help with the wall because I wanted to make her life a little easier.

It felt good to solve a problem that would've taken longer and been harder for her without me.

I know she wants to be independent, but it was a favor.

I'm tall.

Plus, I liked the excuse to spend time with her, to watch her work.

I sent her a text before tip-off to ask how the wall was received by Parker—because it was the right thing to do, not because I can't stand to go back to us not speaking.

"Less showboating, more defense in the second half," Coach demands of everyone before putting in a hand. "Kodiaks on three."

On the way back out, I notice Coach rubbing his chest.

"You good?" I ask.

He drops the hand. "I'll be fine if you all go out there and do your job."

We're back out there, changing ends and paying more attention to their end of the court. Atlas gets a block, and Miles grabs the rebound, hurling the ball toward a sprinting Rookie at the other end.

The crowd erupts.

"Hell yeah." I clap Rookie on the back as we trot toward the other end.

From then on, we're looking to score.

There's a moment when they make a push in the fourth.

But when the final whistle blows, we win by eight.

Back in the locker room, we expect to see Coach happy with the win.

Instead, he's seething.

"Should've been more. And you"—Coach turns to Rookie—"you can't guard, you won't get anywhere in this league."

I step between them. "He scored twenty-five tonight. Back off."

The room goes silent.

"For that, you'll both sit next game," Coach growls.

Rookie and the guys trail out, most of them heading for the gym we always hit after home games.

I'm still staring. "Coach, come on. Don't bench me. It's bad for the team."

"You're right. I'll bench him."

My mouth falls open.

"You're a team. You didn't listen as a team, so the team gets the consequences. This shit might fly with Utah, but it won't work against LA in four months."

I stomp toward the gym after my teammates.

"What happened?" Rookie asks.

"You're benched," I say.

"What?!"

The guys look confused and dejected.

"Enough," I grunt. "This was a win. Treat it like one."

I pull up my phone and send a five-grand transfer to Rookie.

"You did what I said. And you showed up Utah."

His expression brightens.

They get back to their exercises, but I'm still in a bad mood.

Still no response from Nova.

I shove down the disappointment and force myself to go through the workout.

I'm completely focused—until my phone buzzes next to me while I'm doing pull-downs.

It's only my agent congratulating me on the game, and I tell the disappointment to back the fuck off.

"You wanna spot me?" Jay asks.

I step toward him, hovering behind the barbell as he lifts it from the cups.

Miles hollers, grabbing my shoulder. "Brooke wants everyone to go out to Harrison King's club. There's some DJ playing she wants to see."

"Lots of girls?" Rookie asks hopefully, finishing his set and grabbing a water bottle.

"So many. I could have a threesome in the bathroom," Miles comments gleefully, his phone still in his hand. "Wade looks like he could use one of those. Plenty of girls would like you to after how it went down tonight."

"Not in the mood," I grunt. What I need is an ice bath and a massage.

"Is Chloe going?" Rookie asks.

Jay pushes out another rep, grinning through the effort. "She'd chew you up and spit you out."

"She loved the book I got her."

"She was being nice." Jay counters.

"We're doing a buddy read." Rookie's grin turns smug. "If she's thinking of chewing me up and spitting me out, she sure seems to like how I taste."

Jay's face darkens as he grits out his final rep.

Miles types some more, then grins. "Nova's going."

I straighten so fast I nearly drop the barbell Jay passes to me. "How do you know?"

"I asked." He flashes his phone at me so fast I only see her name at the top and bright symbols on the screen.

I don't know if I'm more jealous she's talking to him or that their text chain is full of emojis. Who knew yellow smileys could make me feral?

"You coming?" Miles asks me again.

I yank a clean towel off the shelf and rub it over my face.

"Yeah, I might stop by."

7

NOVA

I scrub the flakes of paint off my skin. Hot water streams over my body, a cozy reward for a job well done.

The team got a win, but I didn't stick around to celebrate. Instead, I went straight back to Brooke's to shower.

When I step out, there's a figure standing in the doorway of the bathroom.

I shriek. "Dammit Brooke! You scared the shit out of me."

"We're going out." She passes me a towel, and I wrap it around myself. Any boundaries about nudity were broken down within the first three days when I realized Brooke is entirely unselfconscious and assumes everyone else is too.

"It's Tuesday."

"Tuesday gets a bad rap. And I got a new advertiser."

"Amazing!" I grab a second towel and wrap it around my damp hair.

"Did James like the pics you sent?"

"He said it's a start." I put the finishing touches on the skyline today, the polishing and shading that made it extra realistic. "Now I need to figure out what's next."

I wipe a spot on the mirror clean of steam and moisturize my face.

The next phase, we agreed, is painting the players in action. I've sketched a few options, but nothing's coming together yet.

Brooke's face appears behind me. "You need inspiration. This club is the hottest thing. I'll let you raid my closet," she promises.

"That's more for you than for me," I say.

"Come on, you're my quirky pink Barbie." Her dark eyes are big and pleading.

The change of scenery could be good. I could use the chance to get out and unwind. Who knows, maybe it will inspire me to figure out the next part of my mural too?

"Deal."

She hooks an arm around my neck and drags me into her room. Inside her closet, she flips through garments, rejecting one after another in a rainbow collection of labels any designer-loving woman would envy.

I grab my phone while she's searching to find a text came in from Miles.

Miles: Novaaaaa, we got a win! Broke their streak and their spirit.

Nova: Congrats! :D

Miles: You have to come out and celebrate.

Nova: That's Brooke's plan.

He sends through a selfie of him grinning in the locker room.

In the background, Clay is changing.

Jesus.

He's dressed only in shorts, reaching over his head to stretch. His body is hard and muscled, tattoos decorating every inch of him.

My throat dries.

It should be illegal for any guy to be that sexy, with or without clothes.

I click out of the picture...

And find myself confronted with the text Clay sent before the game.

Grumpy Baller: How'd James like his masterpiece?

I haven't answered because yesterday messed with my head.

He took so much care helping me with the wall. Listening to me, following my lead. It almost felt like an apology for the past.

But way he grabbed my hand at the end felt very much like the present.

I swear I can still feel his touch.

It doesn't change anything.

It can't.

I need to purge these feelings, show us both I'm over whatever we were.

I drop the phone on her bed and cross to the closet, pointing at a silver shift on a hanger. "How about this one?"

"On a Tuesday?"

"Better to be overdressed than underdressed."

Brooke's eyes mist. "I'm so proud of you."

"Damn. Didn't know the Hadid sisters were making an appearance."

Brooke and I turn to see Miles behind us at the bar, a grin on his handsome face.

Rookie and Jayden are behind him.

We do look good. She's wearing a black tube top and matching skirt that show off her figure. I'm in Brooke's dress that skims my curves and ends mid-thigh. Add my nude heels and my hair falling in waves to my collarbone and I feel sexier than I have in weeks.

The club is packed, though it's barely eleven, the music pulsing through the floor.

The headliner tonight is Little Queen, one of my favorite DJs, though she hasn't taken the stage.

"Did you win?" Brooke asks.

"I'm hurt you didn't check." Miles leans in, his button-down shirt pulling across his muscled form.

"Not as hurt as you would've been if you'd lost to Utah."

He grins. "We won. Clay and Rookie lit 'em up."

Brooke raises a brow. "And you ate popcorn on the sidelines?"

Miles scoffs, surveying the club with a grin. A woman catches his eye, and he nods to her.

"Speaking of, first round's on me. Coach benched me, but Clay covered for me," Rookie goes on, nodding across the club.

I follow his gaze to see Clay shaking hands with a man in a suit.

Clay's gorgeous, head and shoulders above the rest of the crowd, looking like a god in a room of mortals.

The guy in the suit says something, and Clay grins—that slow, reluctant smile that used to make me melt.

For a moment he looks genuine, the guy who put my drawings out in public and who covers for his teammate.

I pull out my phone and start to type out a response to his text.

Except when I look up, a group of women are swarming him, and it's like a bucket of ice over my head.

I delete the message without sending it and turn back to the bar, ignoring the disgust in my stomach.

"Come on, let's dance!" Brooke declares, grabbing my hand and tugging me toward the floor.

I toss back my drink and follow her. We throw ourselves into the music as the alcohol buzzes through my system.

The track changes to Drake, and she throws her hands in the air. With every beat drop, every chorus, every remix, I'm more relaxed.

Especially when we go back for a second drink.

"Who did you tell we were coming tonight?" I whisper-shout in her ear. "Jayden or Miles?"

"Miles. Why?"

I lift a shoulder as I spin in a circle. "Just curious."

I spot him at the bar with Rookie, a blonde and a brunette on either side of them. But Miles is looking toward the dance floor, the smile on his face lingering as he lays eyes on Brooke.

"Did anything ever happen between you two?"

She grabs my arms. "Why do you ask?"

"Because he seems into you."

Brooke rolls her eyes. "He's into himself."

Another guy comes over to dance, and Brooke moves toward him, wrapping her arms around his neck. I go to grab another drink and run into Miles.

"Having fun?" he asks.

"Mhmm. Brooke's brand of fun is contagious."

We both look toward the floor where she's still dancing with the guy. Except now she's scanning the crowd as if she's over it and looking to get away. She walks away, but he follows her.

Miles stiffens at my side. Brooke spots us and cuts our way, the guy still coming after her. Miles steps between them.

"Outta my way," the guy spits. "This doesn't concern you."

"It's about her, it's about me," Miles says, deadly calm.

"Wait, I know you. You're on the Kodiaks."

The guy's grin fades, and he lifts both hands, appreciating how outmatched he is. He accidentally bumps me as he walks away, and I nearly spill my drink, but a hand closes around my wrist, another at my waist.

I look up to see Clay hovering over me.

His hair curls around his ears, still damp from his shower. He's wearing a dark dress shirt, the top button undone. The sleeves are rolled to expose some of the black ink that enthralled me the first time we met.

He's so gorgeous it hurts to look at him.

But as the women in the booth give me dagger eyes, I can't resist engaging.

"You left your fan club," I inform him.

"Not mine."

I cock my head. "Pretty sure if they have your name tattooed on them, they're yours."

He rubs a hand over his face like he's trying to hide a smile.

I shouldn't care. It's a prize in a game I'm no longer playing.

But I'm not in a hurry to get back to Brooke, who's safe with Miles, and Clay doesn't seem like he's in a hurry to go anywhere.

He steps closer, doing a slow inspection of my body. "I like your hair."

"You said that already," I call over the music pulsing through the club.

"Still true."

Alcohol buzzes in my veins, giving me a false sense of bravery. I need all my wits to handle him, but thanks to the two drinks, I'm a little short.

I bite my cheek. "What else do you like?"

Stop flirting, Nova.

But telling myself not to flirt with Clay is like telling myself not to breathe.

His gaze doesn't move from mine. "Like your dress."

Awareness has the hairs on my neck lifting. In this place surrounded by darkness and music and sexy people in sexy outfits, it feels like we're in another world. One where the usual rules don't apply. As if I can say or do anything and it will be forgotten tomorrow.

"Keep going," I say, and his nostrils flare.

"Like your wall. Passed it twice today."

The quickest path to practice and games is going in the back door, which doesn't take him past there. Which means he made an effort to go by my work.

"I'm working on the players next. I wish I had that drawing from the Kodiaks' charity auction as a reference. It should be easy, but sketching you is harder than I remember."

"Wonder why that is."

The song changes to something downtempo. I toss back the drink in my hand in one gulp and set the glass on the bar.

"I thought I saw you. I was wrong."

When I straighten, Clay's watching intently. "Nova. About the wedding—"

"You were right," I interrupt, because I can't

stand to hear him break his stony silence just to tell me all the reasons we'd never happen. "It wouldn't have worked with us. Thank you for seeing it before I did."

Clays brows draw together in a frustrated line.

I hold up a finger for the bartender and order a tequila shot.

"When I said we were nothing, I didn't mean *you* were nothing," he says as the bartender fills the shot glass.

That's not better, because I valued what we had. It was like a tiny blossoming flower, and he crushed it under his Kobes.

I reach for my wallet.

"She with you?" the bartender asks Clay.

Clay nods, and the other man waves my wallet away.

"I'm not..."

They ignore me.

"To dodging bullets," I tell him.

"That what we did?"

My gaze lowers to the ink snaking out from under his shirt.

Cheers erupt as Little Queen takes the stage.

I look out toward the dance floor and see Brooke waving at me.

I reach for my shot glass and the salt.

"Do you want one?" I hold out the drink.

Clay shakes his head. Because he doesn't drink during the season.

Basketball first.

Everything else second, if ever.

No room for weakness or caring about another person.

The Kodashians are still watching, a flock of vultures waiting to see if I'm going to eat my prey or leave some for them.

Except when one of them whispers in the other's ear and they both laugh as they look back at me, it's clear they don't think of me as a threat.

I have the sudden impulse to mark my territory, even if it's not mine anymore.

I reach for Clay's hand, the warmth of his skin making my stomach flip instantly. I spread his thumb and forefinger, shaking salt between them.

Holding his gaze, I suck it off his skin, feeling the jolt of heat between my thighs as I do. When I toss the drink back, the fiery alcohol burns down my throat.

As I slam the shot glass back on the bar, his nostrils flare.

Suddenly, it doesn't feel like I've dodged a bullet.

It feels like I've missed out on something momentous.

I start to turn away, but a hand closes around my wrist, tugging me back. I'm crushed against a hard expanse of muscle and tattoo.

"How many walls?" His mouth is at my ear, more urgent this time.

"What?" My eyes snap up to his.

I should have known better than to think I could call him out, put my mouth on him and not elicit a response.

The feel of him so close is overwhelming me, making my emotions go haywire.

"How many walls do I need to paint for you to forgive me?" His voice is raw, his gaze a thousand miles deep.

I look up at him, not bothering to hide the emotions swirling inside me along with the tequila.

Every part of me aches for him. Even now, his expression says it's only us in this entire club.

Without permission, my hand skims up his chest to his shoulder, my fingers tracing the line of the tattoo beneath his shirt. The one I chose.

But he doesn't want me. He wants forgiveness. Absolution.

Because he's ready to move on with his life, and if I'm smart, I'll find a way to move on with mine.

"Too many," I whisper before pulling away.

8

CLAY

*F*uck, that didn't go the way I planned.

Nova's out on the floor dancing, her hands over her head and her pink hair catching the lights.

My "Kodashians," as she called them, are waving from the booth, swaying together and sending me blatant looks.

The only woman I'm running hot for is the one dancing with Brooke.

I told myself I was coming tonight to prove to her we could coexist.

It backfired.

She wants nothing to do with me, and I'm realizing I can't take a breath without thinking about her.

When I laid eyes on her tonight, it was like taking a charge at full speed. Her bright eyes danced with fire. Her glossy lips had my dick sitting up and taking notice.

She looks like every weakness I've ever denied, her hair falling in cotton candy waves around her shoulders and her dress hugging every curve I never had a chance to memorize with my hands.

Or my tongue.

More than that, she's earnest and fun and so vital it hurts. I'd follow her around on my knees if she asked me to.

We're nothing.

It wasn't true when I wrote it, and it's even less true now.

Pretending I didn't care a month ago was hell. Playing the asshole who hurt her now is worse.

She hates me.

I ache for her.

I wanted the innocent, questioning girl who arrived here, and I want the woman who paints walls and tosses retorts at me now even more.

Sending her away was supposed to save us both, but I'm still in Denver, and it turns out, she didn't need my help.

"Shots?" Jay calls in surprise as I reach for my

untouched tequila. "That's new for you. Thought you were driving."

"Limo's on me."

"You wanna talk about it?"

"Not really."

"Alright." He claps a hand on my shoulder and heads for the dance floor.

I hate the way the alcohol feels burning down my throat, but I'm not about to admit it.

"Don't get into a fight," I tell Miles, referring to the guy he almost hit when I was approaching.

"Because you're the poster boy for following the rules." He smirks.

Of the guys in the Kodiaks, when I need to talk to someone, it's Jay I go to. But since I've been keeping this secret about LA, we don't talk as much as we used to.

He knows there was something going on with me and Nova, just like he knows I haven't wanted to talk about it since she left.

On the other hand, Miles and I have been on the same team for two years, and we've joked around but never talked about anything serious. I respect his talent and work ethic. He looks as frustrated as I feel, nursing a beer and glaring across the crowd.

"What happened on the court tonight?" I ask, for something to do that's not watching Nova.

"I've been working my ass off, pulling double workouts in the gym, but it's not coming together. Rookie comes in, and it's nothing. The guy fucking farts and the ball goes in." He waves with both hands and my mouth twitches.

"You know when you get to a spot on the court and you're half a beat late. The perfect shot's not perfect unless you're there at the right moment."

He eyes me. "You're always there at the right time."

It's against my nature to be self-deprecating—you wanna be the best, you gotta start by believing you are before anyone else does—but Miles needs a cheering section and apparently Jay's been sucked onto the dance floor via some Mariah Carey remix I'm gonna have to have surgically removed from my brain.

So, I say, "I had a rough patch in college. Nothing I did could fix it. My sister was sick, and I took a week out to visit her. At the time, I resented her for taking me out of it."

"That's cold."

Don't I know it.

But I figured the best way I could be there for her was to make it and provide for her.

Now, she's in graduate school, dating a professor who's older than I am, and flips me off anytime I insist on sending her money.

I motion for another shot of tequila.

"Kicker is, the time out helped," I admit. "You can change your arc, your angle, your rotation, but you can't force the perfect timing." I remember the days in the hospital, the group chats about practices I was missing, the increasingly frustrated texts from my coach until I finally caved. "When I came back, my problems were solved."

"All of 'em?"

I take the drink from the bartender and toss it back, feeling the alcohol burn through my system. "Not the acne."

Miles howls with laughter. "You're a decent guy when you're like this. All existential and shit."

The song changes again, the beat vibrating through my shoes as my attention tracks the dance floor.

Alcohol throbs in my bloodstream, the two drinks making me less guarded than usual.

"Are you into Nova?"

If Miles is surprised by the question, he doesn't

show it. He nods to the beat before lifting a shoulder. "She's really cool. What do you want me to say?"

It's my nature to not give a shit about anything.

But I care about this.

"Say no."

Miles laughs. "Fine. But only because it's you."

I exhale, and my gaze tugs back to Nova dancing with Brooke. "You think if you missed your chance to do something, you get another shot?"

"Only if you're smarter the second time around."

9

NOVA

I can't remember the last time I woke up with a hangover. But sure enough, a headache and dry mouth greeted me this morning like an old friend.

I wish I could say I remembered everything that happened last night, but some parts are blurry.

Putting on a fierce dress? Check.

Dancing with Brooke? Check.

Flirting with Clay and possibly crossing a line in the attempt to piss of his Kodashians?

Very possible.

Unfortunately.

By noon, the hangover was mostly gone.

The unease about how I acted lingers.

I'm getting ready to head out to meet Mari and

Harlan for dinner when there's a knock on the apartment door.

I look through the peephole, and all I see is a riot of pink.

Tugging the handle, I cock my head at the delivery guy who peers around his parcel.

"These are for Nova."

No dozen roses, but a hundred ranunculus and gerberas in every shade of pink. They look soft and lush and smell divine.

What the hell?

The bouquet fills my arms, and I carry it over to the kitchen table before pulling out the card.

Forgive me.

CW

My stomach dances.

This wasn't the first gift that arrived today.

Near the end of a day of painting, a nail technician showed up with a portable setup to redo my manicure but wouldn't tell me who sent her.

Clayton Wade isn't the kind of guy to ply a girl with gifts. Especially not fragrant pink ones.

He goes around living his life, giving a hot broody nod to one of the thousands of women ready to drop everything to be on his arm or in his bed for a night.

But the cut stems exploding across the table beg to differ.

How many walls do I need to paint?

The stubborn longing I hoped I'd kicked starts up again.

Last night, I swore he was only trying to soothe his guilty conscience.

But this feels like something else entirely.

I ignore the pleasant buzzing in my stomach and sneak a last look at the flowers before I head out the door for real.

"How's the project going?" Mari asks me when we're settled at the restaurant.

"The skyline is looking fantastic," Harlan adds.

When Mari texted to suggest dinner tonight, I jumped at it because I want to rebuild my relationship with my sister. Since I got back to Colorado, I've seen her twice for coffee. The last time, she was more interested in who I was dating—no one, I'd emphasized—than our relationship.

She asked if Harlan could come too, and I was only a little disappointed. He's a good guy, and now he's family.

"Thank you. The skyline is actually done, and I'm starting on the next part. I figured you'd be on top of it given how interested James is in this anniversary gala."

Harlan tilts his head. "James and I have different roles."

"And styles." I lean in, buttering my bread. "I'm guessing you don't have a diamond watch that looks heavy enough to bludgeon your enemies with."

Harlan's mouth twitches as he reaches for his wine.

"Is he really as much of a 'my way or the highway' guy as he seems?" I ask.

"More," Harlan says.

I laugh, but it's unsettling to be working for a person with that reputation.

"May I take the extra place setting?" the waitress asks.

"Sure," I say, but Mari holds up a hand.

"No, he's running behind. There he is!"

A tingle of dread climbs up my spine. I turn to see a guy in a sport coat striding toward us, his wide, white smile blinding.

"This is Paul. He works with me," Mari says.

"Hi, Paul." I plaster on a smile.

"Neat hair," he says as he takes the empty seat opposite me.

"Thank you."

"It's pink," he goes on, folding the napkin tidily in his lap without taking his eyes off me.

I try to match his wide smile. "It is."

Mari kicks me under the table, and I remind myself to play nice.

The four of us make conversation, and I resist the urge to throttle my sister for setting me up on a blind date. I make it until our appetizers are done, while the guys are talking about sports—apparently Paul's more into golf than basketball—and Mari rises to use the bathroom.

I follow her in.

"Really? A date?" I demand when she emerges from the stall to wash her hands.

"Brad's been out of the picture for months. You need a boyfriend."

"Mar, I don't need to be taken care of."

She flips her palms. "Maybe you want

someone. I love being with Harlan. He's smart and handsome. He props me up when I'm down and calls me on my bullshit when I'm talking crap."

"Let me guess—you can't remember life without him?" I tease.

Mari smiles and rolls her eyes. "I know it's nuts because we met less than a year ago, but I don't want to," she says softly.

My heart flips over. It's sweet, what they have. The way he looks out for her, challenges her, champions her. I wish I could tell her that I met a guy who makes me feel that way.

"Just give Paul a chance, okay? He works on accounts, and he's a nice guy."

"All right," I promise and head back out with her.

Paul looks up, white teeth flashing as I sit. "There you are. We were going to send out a search party."

I take a deep breath. "No need. We made it back alive."

He tosses back his head and laughs. The sound echoes off the walls.

The man laughs at nearly everything. It should be a refreshing change.

Somehow, it's not.

There's no grumpy side-eye. No jaw-twitching, no hand-flexing.

Definitely no groping under the table.

Still, as our main courses arrive, I vow to do as I promised.

"So, what brought you to Denver?" Paul asks as he digs into his salmon.

I fill him in on my project, and his brows rise.

"It's a big painting on a wall. People will touch it with their sticky fingers?" He frowns.

"I guess? But art exists to be enjoyed."

Harlan clears his throat. "Any thoughts on what else besides the skyline?"

"I'm still working on it." I think back to last night. I didn't get the stroke of specific inspiration Brooke suggested, but I got a feeling. More of a vibe.

Everyone together, the Kodiaks, working toward a common goal.

I couldn't sleep when I got home, so I sketched. I could do most of them from memory and photo references.

But I couldn't do Clay.

Not his broad shoulders, the tattooed expanse of him.

Not his chiselled jaw.

Not his aggressive stance.

Not those dark eyes that see everything.

A buzzing sound comes from my bag hanging on the back of my chair. I try to be subtle as I reach for it, but Mari pins me with a look.

"Could be Brooke," I mouth, but I slip the phone into my lap and glance at it.

Grumpy Baller: Did you get the flowers?

I ignore the text and return to the conversation, but a minute later, my phone rings.

I jump up, three sets of surprised eyes flying my way.

"I'm so sorry. Give me one minute."

I dash for the hall, the *Grumpy Baller* contact on the screen making me curse.

"Clay, this is not a good time," I answer once I'm tucked out of sight.

"So, you don't like the flowers," he deadpans.

In the restaurant full of strangers flirting and clinking wine glasses, his voice is more real than any of it.

I sigh. "They're beautiful. But they can't erase the past."

"That's not what I wanted to do." There's a

long pause. "I've been thinking about you a lot. I guess I wanted you to think of me."

The laughter bubbles up from nowhere. "Trust me, thinking of you isn't my problem." I should stop talking, but the words spill out. "I spend my day on a ladder with a twenty-foot-high image of you at my back. Which makes it even more fucked up that I can't draw you, because I know every inch of you."

"Not every inch." His voice lowers, and suddenly I'm reminded of everything we did.

And all the things we didn't.

"Goodnight, Clay—"

"Wait, don't hang up." His breathing gets louder. "The night of the wedding, I should have taken you home with me. God knows I wanted to."

My head falls back, and I stare unseeing at the overhead lights. "Then why didn't you?" I can't help asking.

"Because I fucked up. I cared about you, Nova. I still care."

The emotion in my chest is twisting, agonizing, but it's not the emptiness of the past month. There's a glimmer of light beneath it all.

Hope.

But he didn't take me home, I remind myself as

a woman brushes past me heading for the bathroom. Instead, he gave me a letter that made me feel an inch tall.

Paul might not be the guy for me, but I need someone who understands how to act like a grown-up. How to communicate and compromise.

Clay has a million pieces of evidence as to why he's amazing. I'm still trying to prove to myself that I have my life figured out.

"I need to make this mural for James incredible," I say at last. "You want to make it up to me, help me not be hung up on yesterdays that can't exist again. Help me live my life now."

"Nova—"

"I'm on a date," I choke out before I click off and switch my phone to "do not disturb".

I head back to the table, uttering my apologies as I shove the device back in my bag.

The rest of dinner is a grind.

Paul asks for my number, and I give it to him mostly to help him save face in front of Mari and Harlan.

I get home to find Brooke still out and the entire apartment smelling like a field of wildflowers.

I cross to the bouquet, and my fingers reach for the petals of one, stroking their velvety surface.

They're beautiful. Fresh and bright and happy.

A knock at the door makes me jump.

What the...?

It's not someone from outside the building, or the concierge would have buzzed up. Maybe Brooke forgot her key?

When I pull the door open, there's a security guard standing in the hallway holding a large rectangle wrapped in brown paper.

"I brought a message from Mr. Wade."

"I'm afraid I've hit my limit of messages from Mr. Wade for tonight."

I start to shut the door, but he holds out the package. The size and shape of it are immediately familiar.

I take it from him and shut the door before reading the Post-It note on top.

To help you live your life.

10

CLAY

"*A*gain?!?" Rookie exclaims as Miles's three swishes into the hoop.

It's Miles's fifth of the night, and my teammate's grin lasts the whole way back up the court. The crowd is going nuts. We're up big, and the third-string guys pop off the bench to close.

Miles pants next to me on the bench as we catch our breath in the final minute.

It wasn't a record game, but I still got mine, and after the other night, I know how much this was eating Miles.

But my lungs burn, and it's not from running up and down the court.

When Nova said there was no number of walls

that would make her forgive me, it didn't discourage me.

It lit a fire under me.

So first, I sent her a manicurist to fix the nails she was upset about.

Next were flowers. The universal symbol for "I fucked up, hope these make you smile when I couldn't."

I could've handled her cursing me out.

What I got in return was a thousand times worse.

"I'm on a date."

It felt like taking a charge from a power forward barreling downhill toward the basket.

All the air went out of me at once, leaving every part of me bruised.

Being around her the past two weeks has brought me back to life. Seeing her pursue her dreams in the hallway outside, hearing her laughter, brushing against her at the club, all of it reminds me how she lights me up like no one I can remember.

I won't pretend not to have feelings for her anymore.

But what if it's too late?

Maybe Nova's over us, and I'm the one left holding onto something we won't have again.

After hitting the showers and media, I get dressed in jeans and a sweater. My hair is still wet, and it feels cool in the November air as I step outside.

"Leave the car," Miles says as the limo comes to pick us up.

"Where we going, Vegas?" Jay demands.

When I shift inside, Brooke is already there.

Plus Nova.

She's wearing jeans and a cropped white T-shirt that makes me think of all the ways I'd get her dirty.

My heart lifts for the first time all day. A surge of anticipation and adrenaline pumps through me.

She knew I'd be here. So, why is she? Especially after her "back off, I'm on a date" call last night.

"Hey." I shift into the seat beside her, my legs extending across the floor.

"Hi." Nova's tongue darts out to lick her lips. "Thank you for the picture."

"Sure."

She chews on her lip, and I want to tug it from between her teeth.

"You had it this entire time," she says quietly enough only I can hear. "The person who bought it at the auction before anyone could... that was you."

So, that's what this is about.

Miles drops onto her other side before I can respond. "I was on fire tonight."

"You were okay," Nova teases.

Miles nods toward the door next to Brooke, and she passes him a bottle of water without either of them exchanging a word.

The entire ride over, the car is filled with joking and laughter.

There's no space for me and Nova to talk, so we don't.

But she looks edgy, her fingers playing with her hair.

When the car pulls up, we spill out in a line and into the pub.

Some locals are in there, and cheers go up when we arrive. The guys and I make the rounds, slapping high fives and fist bumps with the regulars.

"Looking good, Miles."

"How's the knee, Wade?"

"Hell of a steal, Jay."

I look up too late to see my teammates are

already settling into our round booth, Nova first and Miles piling in after her. Brooke's on her other side. By the time I make it there through the crowd congratulating me, only the outside seat is left.

The waitress is on us immediately, getting our order. I get a Coke, and most of the guys opt for soda too, except Miles, who gets shots.

A couple of women come over and ask if they can join us. One takes the side next to Jay and the other next to me.

After a few drinks, the girl next to Jay rises. "Dance with me?"

He agrees, letting her drag him to the floor.

Another woman comes up, already eyeing me.

She cups her hands around my ear and leans in. "I'll dance however you want me to. You don't have to move. You can be a sexy pole."

I feel Nova's eyes on us.

I'm about to say no, until Miles stands.

"Come on, beautiful," he says to Nova. "I need someone to hold me up."

I expect her to decline, but she's rising, letting him thread his hand in hers.

Atlas clears out of the far side to let them through. I watch Miles tug Nova toward the dance floor.

"This isn't happening, is it?"

"Huh?"

I force myself to look at the woman who asked me to dance.

"That's what I thought." She smiles. She's objectively attractive, but I couldn't care less. "Still gonna tell everyone I've ever met that I danced with Clayton Wade, if that's okay?"

"Knock yourself out."

I watch Miles and Nova dance, mostly to punish myself.

Maybe she is over me.

I've never been one to accept defeat. I'll go down fighting and bloody first. But I can't stand the idea of her being collateral damage again. Not when I've already hurt her.

I told myself she was better off, that what mattered most to her was going back to the life she left behind.

But she's here, living her best life inches away, and all I want is to be part of it.

Brooke's voice cuts in. "Chocolate."

I glance over to find her at my side. "Huh?"

"First year of college, I went on this diet. I'd never really restricted what I ate before, but I was trying to fit in at my sorority, and that was how a lot of the girls ate. The way you're looking at her is how I looked at chocolate all semester."

I exhale hard. "You don't know shit, Brooke."

"She talks about you in her sleep."

My head cranks around.

"The other night, I went into her room, and she was talking about you."

I turn back to the dance floor, competing feelings raging inside me.

She still thinks about me.

Fuck, she *dreams* about me.

Mr. Thirty Points loops an arm around Nova's waist and leans in to whisper at her ear.

Every muscle in my body tightens.

I'm out of my seat and beside them in three steps. My hand closes around her wrist, my grip swallowing up her small arm.

Without a word, I pull her after me.

NOVA

The smell of beer and fried foods permeates the air, but it's overrun by the scent of his body wash and him as he pushes me up against one of the shelves filled with cardboard boxes.

The walls of the storeroom press in on me. So does Clay's body, filling my vision.

"You can't toss me around. I'm not a basketball," I complain.

"Why'd you come out tonight?" His face is bent so he's inches from mine, his gaze pinning me.

"To hang out with friends."

"But you knew I'd be here."

"I'm not avoiding you for the rest of my time in Denver."

"Brooke heard you talking about me in your dreams."

Oh boy.

I already feel a step behind when it comes to this man. Brooke's help to tip the scales in his favor is overkill.

"I talk a lot in my sleep," I say defensively. "About all kinds of—"

"I don't think so, Pink."

My jaw hangs open.

Tonight, I went to the game because I told myself it would help me sketch the team for my mural. But my eyes kept dragging back to Clay. He was so intentional, deliberate, powerful. Flying back and forth up the court, cutting between defenders, taking everything he wanted.

I know what he's gone through with his knee, the struggle about going to LA, and he keeps it all inside.

He's a mess of contradictions.

Finding out he had that picture threw me because it meant not only did he support my work by buying it for an exorbitant price, but he was somehow responsible for it showing up in a top magazine.

He said in his letter that he didn't care, but his actions since have proved otherwise.

His actions keep proving otherwise.

"Someone in here?"

An unfamiliar voice at the door makes us stiffen.

Clay spins to hide my body from whoever's entering.

"Oh, Wade. Thank you again for the check last week. I wouldn't still be in business without you."

When the man shuts the door after him, I can breathe again.

My hands fist in the back of Clay's sweater. "What was that about?"

He turns to stare me down.

"Because it sounds like you helped that man save his bar," I go on, digging a finger into his muscled chest. "*This* is your problem. You barely say two words, and it leaves people to think the worst of you."

Clay shifts on his feet. "It was nothing."

I fold my arms and glare up at him. "Everything is nothing with you."

"You with another guy isn't nothing." His teeth grind together as he leans over me. "Miles. Whoever took you out the other night. They're not good enough for you."

"And you are?"

He grabs my chin and kisses me hard.

His lips are hot and firm, his body bending mine around the metal post between my shoulders. I want to tell him to back off, but the scorching heat of his mouth, the grip of his fingers, sends electricity through me that I haven't felt in weeks.

It's wrong, but it's so good, and I kiss him back.

My hands fist the sweater at his waist, the hard muscles bunching beneath my touch.

What Miles leaned over to tell me was that his good game was thanks to Clay.

Everything comes back to him.

He takes the move as consent and leans in.

The last weeks without him piled up like a crushing weight, and now that he's so close, all I want is to lose myself in his grumpy embrace.

When he wedges his knee between my parted thighs, I move against him. My back arches, and my hips undulate of their own accord, pressing against his leg.

He licks between my lips and grabs the waistband of my jeans. The zipper gives way as he yanks it down.

Clay shoves the fabric off my hips and down my legs, dragging my thong with it. Then a hand is between my thighs.

"Miles plays backup for me, sweetheart." His voice is a rasp as his lips drag across my cheek, his teeth nipping at my ear. "I know you didn't get this wet for him."

But I can't be embarrassed when he plunges two fingers inside me, hard and deep. The touch ignites me, and I try and fail to swallow a moan.

His fingers thrust, proving his point.

I need to feel his skin without all these clothes.

My hands sneak up under his sweater. His skin is hot and smooth, satin over ridges of hard-won muscle.

He groans. "Say you came back for me. For us."

My heart kicks.

None of it makes sense. He's the one who broke things off.

But it's impossible to think when he's pumping in and out, long strokes that push me to the limit. My body welcomes him as though he never left, as though every day was a tick mark on a cell wall while I waited for him to return and set me free.

He rubs the sweet spot inside that makes me convulse.

"Wait," I say.

Clay pulls back an inch, our breath still mingling in pants.

"You told me the next time you made me come, it wouldn't be on your fingers."

His eyes gleam.

He spins me around and bends me over, forcing me to grab the post for balance as he spreads me wide.

His lips brush down my back, my thighs.

Oh God.

I want this. I've wanted him for so long.

He licks a strip from the top of my pussy all the way back.

It's so good it hurts. I'm in physical pain from

how tight I'm strung, my core begging for a release I know deep down only he can give me.

"Beautiful girl. Bet you're aching for me to fill you up right now."

I want to touch him, but in this position, I can't reach.

His muscled arms wrap around the tops of my thighs and hold me in place.

Clay teases me with his tongue, slicking across my skin and diving inside.

He spreads me wider, exposing every inch of me to his attention.

"The things I've imagined doing when I had you like this," he murmurs.

The past month, I've tried not to think of him when I'm alone in bed touching myself.

But it's always him.

It's impossible to imagine someone else when I've been with him.

Still, he doesn't fill me with anything except his tongue, and even that strays inside for only a second before returning to my clit and my folds.

It's maddening.

My moan spills out, the sounds of my pleasure echoing off the walls.

My fingers flex on the post, my toes curling in my shoes.

It's as if his only mission in life right now is to make me feel him, to want him. Only him. Always him.

I never thought I'd be getting tongue-fucked by an all-star against a shelf in the back of a pub. But then, I've grown a lot this fall.

I arch my back, inviting him.

My fingers let go of the post and I reach back to grab his shoulder, twisting to try and look at him.

"You're so sweet on my tongue," he groans. "You'd be even sweeter on my cock."

His expression is feral, the tattoos on his forearms like devils coming out to play as he grips me.

The pleasure builds until I'm out of my mind with need. My vision blurs.

He sucks me one more time, punishingly long and deep on a low groan that fills the room.

Ecstasy explodes through my body, each nerve firing off sparks of pure bliss that threaten to consume me completely.

His arms wrap around me, pulling me close in a desperate embrace from behind.

We don't speak, just hold each other.

I'm wrecked, but in some ways, this feels inevitable.

"Turn around." He murmurs it as my heart rate comes back down.

I do. My pants are still around my ankles, my face flushed.

I'm shaking from the orgasm, but the air still crackles between us.

He looks at me with an intensity that takes my breath away.

We're not done, I realize as he reaches into his pants and pulls out his cock.

And wow.

He's huge and thick, and I never thought a dick could be beautiful, but I was wrong.

"Quit trying to distract me with compliments," he growls.

"I didn't say a word."

"You did with your eyes."

"It wasn't a compliment. I'm just surprised you're not tattooed there."

He half laughs, half coughs. "I'm not that stupid."

My lips twitch too, until he drops his other hand between my thighs and draws a gasp from me.

His touch is there only long enough to coat his fingers with my wetness.

Then he grips his cock.

My throat dries.

Clay's hand drags down, his length throbbing against his merciless grip.

Holy.

Again.

It's the hottest thing I've ever seen.

Again.

"Don't move," he rasps.

I couldn't if the room was on fire.

A few hard strokes and he's grunting in time with his motions.

It's the same way he moves on the court, only sexier. He's private and ruthless, chasing his own pleasure inches from where he made me come harder than I ever have moments ago.

His dark eyes capture mine, and I can't breathe. I feel the battle raging inside him.

"Nova..."

His jaw works, and I breathe along with him. I reach up, my fingers stroking the side of his face.

"Don't stop," I whisper.

He comes on a groan, coating my thighs and stomach.

It's beyond sexy, watching this man who's sacrificed everything his entire life for a single purpose lose control with me. On me.

Clay straightens his clothes, then turns to mine. He's careful with me, tugging up my thong, my jeans.

He doesn't clean me up first. The fabric sticks to my skin like a filthy secret.

He pulls me close, pressing his lips against my forehead.

"Whoever he is, I'll always look better on you than he does."

11

CLAY

"You gotta have a signature move," Miles insists to Rookie. "The last three winners have a move. They get you votes."

Rookie does a crossover, then flips the ball behind his back and up for a dunk.

"The fuck was that?!" Coach demands.

"I need a signature move. For Rookie of the Year."

"Signature move is gonna be my foot in your ass." Coach lowers his voice, but we can still hear him, and Jay buries his laugh in a cough. "You want gold statues, kid? Contribute on a team, you get paid. Then you buy all the gold you want."

Coach blows his whistle, and a different group

takes the floor, Jayden bringing the ball up from half court.

I'm distracted, but sue me.

Rookie rubs a towel over his head and comes over to me. "I can't do this. Whenever I try to do something big, I get slapped down."

"You gotta serve your time when you get drafted."

"You didn't. You were shot out of a cannon with a grudge."

I shake my head because he's not wrong. "This sport is a long game. Be smart about it."

"Like last night with Nova?" he asks, and my head snaps around. "I went looking for y'all and heard you."

Hooking up in the back room of the bar wasn't planned, but fuck did I need it.

Watching her flirt with Miles broke my control, especially when Brooke informed me that Nova's "I'm over you" act was exactly that.

When I dragged her back to the storeroom, I wasn't sure if I wanted to curse her or take her over my knee.

What I needed most was to taste her. To make her moan my name. To prove to myself I still could.

She wants me. That much is clear.

The way she came on my face, the sounds she made, the way she tasted—it's all gonna live rent free in my head a long damn time.

Jerking off to her, with her, was the only way I could keep from bending her over and fucking her right there while she was still trembling.

It was the hottest experience of my life.

Kicker is, it's not enough.

Not nearly.

We run the next sequence, and I'm a step behind to defend, so I have to catch up.

I take Rookie out of the air, and he lands hard on his back.

"Fuck," he grunts from the ground.

"My bad," I murmur as I hold out a hand and help him up after.

I glance up to see Harlan waiting in the wings, watching silently, hands in the pockets of his suit pants.

"You ever ditch the suit?" I cross to him, tugging on my shorts. "These things might put a little swing back in your step."

"You think you don't have a stick up your ass? Anyone tried to get up in your routine, they'd face the same kind of resistance. We're not as dissimilar as you like to think."

I'm trying not to think too hard on that when he goes on.

"He's good," Harlan says, nodding to Rookie. "It's one thing for you to demand a trade, but don't burn the place down on your way out."

I stiffen. "You don't see me helping him out?"

"I see you taking him out at the knees, giving him the same injury as you."

My hands ball into fists. I've been working with Rookie all the time, but Harlan takes one look and decides he knows what's up.

"For a man who thinks he sees everything, you don't see shit." This is why we can't work together. I grimace. "I want an update on our deal."

"LA's got some issues, and we've had complications on this end too."

"My stock is up. I'm averaging twenty-eight a night. We have a winning record."

He rocks back on his heels. "Wins and losses aren't the only complication around here. Tenth anniversary's a big deal." He shakes his head. "James is richer than God, and he's decided this is his time to put his mark on the organization whether it needs it or not, which means we're all tasked with making it happen. The regular operations of the team are second to the spectacle."

Harlan clears his throat. "I know it's not easy keeping up your end of the deal."

The digging in my stomach could be guilt.

I return to my seat, turning over the fact he thinks I'm still keeping my distance from Nova.

Pretty sure he would agree that making his sister-in-law scream in the back room of Mile High is not within the terms of our agreement.

If I got any closer to her than I was last night, we'd be made of the same damn atoms.

But what kind of fucked-up deal dictates relationships between people?

He shouldn't have asked me to do it. I shouldn't have said yes. It's that simple.

"Hey, Rookie," I mutter, and he glances over. "Don't say anything about Nova."

"To the guys?"

"To anyone."

Rookie starts to open his mouth, then closes it again.

NOVA

I'm curled up in a chair at Brooke's place working on a sketch of Clay using my last drawing as a reference. But every time I start, I'm distracted by what happened between us.

"Bet you're aching for me to fill you up right now."

"I'll always look better on you than he does."

My throat is drier than a desert.

I jump up to get a soda from the kitchen, setting my sketchpad and the original drawing on the coffee table and ignoring the tingling between my thighs. I'm trying to make progress on this new section of the mural. Touching myself in the shower and picturing Clayton Wade while I do it doesn't help.

When the phone rings, I change direction, grateful for the interruption.

Mari.

"I'm sorry if the date thing the other night was weird," my sister says when I answer the phone.

"It's fine. I'm not really looking for any kind of relationship."

"This still about Brad?"

"No. I'm trying to focus on my head right now and not my heart." Or the desire flooding me since the other night. The feeling of Clay's tongue inside me, the feel of him coating my skin, haunted me well after Brooke and I got home and I showered off the last evidence of our tryst.

If I'm honest, that grumpy basketball player has been occupying my brain since the moment he tried to evict me from my airplane seat.

"Anyway, what's up?" I prompt.

"You sounded edgy when I texted. Very Un-Nova-like."

I'm surprised she noticed.

"It's work," I admit as I retrieve an open bottle of wine from the fridge. "I want to do my best, and I can't stand the thought of letting James down."

I've never had such an important job.

Yes, what I did in the past mattered, but this is entirely on me.

"Anytime you have a new client, there's a learning curve. Figuring out what matters to them can be hard and painful."

I nod even though Mari can't see me.

"Sometimes you need to fake it until you make it, you know? Pretend you have it all figured out until you really catch up."

"Thank you," I say and mean it.

After we click off, I pour myself a glass of wine and head back to the living room, taking in the drawing Clay sent me before I sink back into my chair.

"I can do this," I say out loud.

It's my first real art commission, but James hired me for a reason.

The irony is the man who gave me this drawing, the same one I'm trying to capture, would agree. He would let nothing stand between him and his goal. And he wouldn't let anyone tell him he wasn't enough.

Two hours and two glasses of wine later, I have a happy buzz in my head and the sketch looks great.

That was exactly what I needed, I decide.

I'm capable and confident, riding a high fueled by achievement and alcohol.

Since I'm finished with the original drawing, I should probably return it.

It's only neighborly.

I grab the picture, put on shoes, and head out into the hall to the elevator.

Two minutes later, I'm staring at the closed door inches from my face, and damn if it doesn't feel as if it's staring back.

My grip tightens, the picture frame digging into my hand to remind me why I'm here.

Just do it.

I'm still deciding whether to lift my knuckles and rap on the wood when the door swings open.

"You gonna stand there all night?" Clay drawls from the other side.

He's wearing a pair of grey sweats resting low on his hips and nothing else. Black ink curls around his muscled arms, over his pecs and abs. His feet are bare. His hair sticks up in every direction in a way that's sexy and messy, and he looks as if he just rolled out of bed.

My throat dries.

How did he...?

There's a lens in the peephole. A camera.

Of course Clay would have security.

Music drifting into the hall has me snapping to attention. It didn't occur to me he was here with someone, but seeing his state of semi-clothedness, a ribbon that feels suspiciously like jealousy snakes up my spine and curls in my stomach.

"I didn't mean to interrupt."

Clay leans against the door frame, folding those bulging arms. "I'm alone."

Satisfaction edges in around the sharp needles, but I play it cool. "I meant you jerking off."

His eyes dance. "You offering to relieve me?"

Heat blooms between my thighs. My body responds whether I want it to or not. He has a direct line to my arousal, a silky rope he tugs on with every smirk, every tilt of his dark head, every rough word from his filthy mouth.

"I came to return this." I hold up the picture.

"That all you came for?" His voice lowers with innuendo, and my attention drags down to the bulge in his pants without warning.

I force my eyes up to meet his.

Clay turns and heads inside, leaving me staring after him, my jaw on the floor, the picture still in my hands.

I follow him inside, the door clicking closed smoothly at my back.

He pads barefoot across the carpet to the living room, where he's watching basketball. I lean the picture carefully against the wall opposite him.

"We need to talk," he says solemnly.

I'm suddenly on guard. "About what happened between us?"

"No. About how much you're getting paid by the Kodiaks."

I frown. "It's none of your business."

"Show me your contract."

He's being bossy, but I'll get out of here faster if I do it. I pull out my phone and open the contract.

He takes my phone and crosses to the living room, sinking onto the huge couch. I follow him, perching on the edge just far enough away we're not touching.

Watching him read all that fine print as if he's ready to shred it is strangely sexy.

"There's nothing about merchandise," he notes when he's done.

"Merchandise? I'm painting a wall. There's not going to be a mascot." I inch closer, trying to read upside down. I give up and shift next to him, peering over his shoulder.

"James will sell this work with the team's name on it."

"That's his right."

"And it's yours to get compensated for it. Every time someone uses my face, my name, I get paid."

"Every time?" I echo. That's staggering. "You can't control when someone draws you. You didn't know when I did."

"You think I didn't know you were watching me?"

"I was discreet."

"Bullshit." He grabs my thighs and drags me

into his lap to straddle him. My hands grip his shoulders for balance. "You looked at me with those big, blue eyes—"

"I did not!" Indignation rises up, and I try without success to wrestle out of his grip. "What does that have to do with my contract?"

"Nothing. I want people to get what they deserve."

"And I deserve more than what I'm making?" I'm treading carefully because I also respect his experience in this industry.

"Way fucking more."

He tucks the phone in the waistband of my shorts.

I take a breath, trying to focus on his words and not his hands settling on my hips, the thumbs brushing absently right above my waistband.

"But I already signed the deal."

"I'll have my agent take a second look."

I bite my lip. "You'd do that?"

"Of course."

Now I'm staring at the subtle print of the couch behind his head because it's easier to think when I'm not looking into his beautiful eyes.

"Why? What is it you want?"

"You," he says roughly, and my heart flips.

"Spent a good long time fighting it. Seems we both got hurt. So, figured I'd try something new."

My throat is dry, my pulse hammering.

Clay is a man who's used to taking what he wants without asking for it. Hearing him say the words makes me tremble.

I'm still drawn to him. I can't get through the day without thinking of what he's doing, who he's with, without missing his grumpy presence or slow, grudging smile.

I want to give this thing between us another chance.

But I won't throw myself at him again. I know better now.

"The picture was in *Architectural Digest*, but the place wasn't yours," I say.

"I loaned it to a friend for a week."

"And it just happened to be when they were shooting *AD*," I press.

He lifts a shoulder.

Dammit.

"Why do you believe in me?" I ask.

"I believe in you the same way I believe the sun's gonna rise and the basketball season's gonna start in October. You're legit. Your talent, your heart, all of it. You're the real deal, Pink."

My ribs are already so stretched it's impossible to take another breath.

God, these feelings are confusing while I'm straddling him in his apartment.

"So then why did you tell me we were over?" I ask quietly.

"I fucked up." Clay frowns, looking uncomfortable. "Things were going so well that I freaked out."

"That makes no sense."

He sighs. "The last time I cared about someone, it went south fast. I looked like a fool, but more than that, it messed me up on the inside. When I get messed up, there's nowhere to hide."

The hope is back, the sneaky spark of possibility deep in my chest.

There's music in the background, but the sound of my pulse pounding is louder. I feel his eyes on me, intent.

"I blocked every mention of you in my search engine so I didn't have to see stories or pictures of you," I blurt.

His touch skims up my ribs. "Seems fair."

"I burned your jersey."

"You..." He shakes his head, eyes closing for a moment. "Fuck it, I'll get you another."

"I still have the letter you dumped me with."

"You're a pyro, it seems, so put it to good use."

I bite my cheek as laughter rises up. "The other night at the pub didn't change anything, you know. Your monster dick didn't rock my world."

"Only because you haven't felt it inside you yet."

The tingling between my thighs intensifies.

"I'm not sure it would even fit."

"You can take me. It'll feel good when you do."

I cock my head. "For you or me?"

"For both of us." Clay twists a piece of my hair around his finger, and his gaze drops to my lips. "Promise I'll go slow."

I'm aware of how close we are, the places we're touching.

I want him so badly I ache.

"I can't jump back into this with you. I need time to listen to my heart. And it's hard to hear it with you right here between my legs, making everything seem like a good idea. Okay?"

He nods slowly, his eyes dancing.

Even if we did start over, it would have to be something new.

Different.

The idea lights up the back of my brain.

I start to shift off him and my phone slips. I grab for it and look at the contract again.

New and different.

"That's it!" I exclaim, pressing a hand against his chest. "I'm adding to the original concept. I could make the case that the changes aren't covered by the contract."

His fingers dig into my bare thigh. "Then what?"

I blink at him. "Then I'll ask for more."

But my words sound weak even to my own ears. I can't picture asking James for more money.

"Based on what?" he levels immediately.

When Clay's fingers find the wide leg of my shorts and slide up the inside, I hiccup.

I should be stopping him. I know what happens when I let my guard down with Clay.

"Based on how much merchandise you sell in the Bear Cave every night, you'd make more than that in a week."

Instead of looking satisfied, the lines on his forehead deepen. *Wrong answer.*

"Actually, probably more than that in a day," I amend. I was always decent enough with numbers to calculate in my head. "And fans love new concepts."

His eyes meet mine, and something in them makes me shiver. I'm getting bolder and more shameless with each breath, and it excites him.

I feel powerful, and it's a strange and heady thing.

"How much did you make this year?" I toss.

He lifts a shoulder. "Forty mil. Give or take."

I try not to faint at the outrageous number.

"Then I'm already winning," I decide.

"How do you figure?" His voice is husky.

"Well." I gesture to our relative positions. "You make forty million dollars... but I'm the one on top."

I swear his grin lights me up everywhere.

12

NOVA

J check my watch for the third time as I shift in the chair outside James Parker's office.

"It's a busy day," the woman at the desk says semi-apologetically. She picks up her phone and punches a contact. "Yes, sir. Nova's here." Her gaze flicks to mine. "Yes, of course." Her finger punches a button—mute, probably, from the way she addresses me at full volume. "He sends his apologies but says it would be best if you continued working on the wall."

"I'm afraid I can't move forward until we talk."

Her lips purse, and she presses the button again. Before she can answer, the door swings open and the owner's head appears.

"Nova. Please come in."

The one and only time I negotiated for my salary at the design firm, they turned me down, citing budget issues. But it left me feeling as if I didn't matter, as if my work didn't matter.

The first week here, I was so worried about messing up that it never occurred to me I wasn't getting my share.

Talking with Clay helped me see how I can advocate for myself, in a way that's fair and reasonable, even in unfamiliar territory.

He holds the door wide, and I follow him inside.

"Would you like a chair?"

"No, thank you." I produce the sketchpad.

Last night after getting back from Clay's, Brooke found me scouring the internet for public rates for commissioned works. When I told her what I was doing, she was immediately supportive.

"Get yours, Nova. You're insanely talented, and you should know your worth."

Now, I watch James take in the sketch.

"What is this?"

"The expanded scope of the wall. You said the board liked the direction with the skyline, but it will be more meaningful to have different levels of connection. The buildings represent Denver, but the players represent basketball, the faces are this team. Your team."

"In that case, I'm impressed. And I approve." He passes the sketchpad back, and I take it.

"I didn't come only for your approval. You offered me twenty thousand for this project. I want twenty more, plus a cut of merchandise."

His brows lift, as do the corners of his mouth. Amused isn't the reaction I was going for, and I grip the edges of my sketchpad tighter, ignoring the urge to tug on my skirt like a school kid in the principal's office.

He rounds the desk, shifting a hip onto the corner, his eyes never leaving mine. "Did you ever take economics, Nova?"

"Yes."

Half a course in community college that I slept through because I was working during the days too.

"Then you know that a person's worth doesn't have anything to do with what they create. It's about the market value. What they can command elsewhere."

I don't like where this is going.

"Is there a competing offer on your time?" he

goes on. "From another employer or patron perhaps?"

He's boxing me into a corner without moving a muscle.

Clay and the other players do their work with their bodies, sleek chess pieces moving around a hardwood board. This man does it with his mind.

I shake my head slowly.

"Then you'll understand why I'm not looking to renegotiate. Besides," he goes on, straightening his tie, "this is good exposure for you. You should be grateful for the project."

"I am grateful, but..."

"Yes?"

My mind spins. "Competing offers work both ways."

He frowns, cocking his head.

I continue. "If I don't finish this, you need to find someone else who will. Can you honestly tell me there's another artist who can work in your timeline and deliver this degree of execution?"

His eyes narrow. "There are always motivated people."

I glance back toward the entrance, the heavy wood. "Did you pick that door?"

"I did. Cherry, imported from quite a distance. Appearances matter."

"How many people come through that door every day? Ten? Twenty?" I lift a shoulder. "That's only for the door of your office. This will be the front door of your organization. Twenty thousand people every night." His eyes glint, and I know I've hooked him. "If you're questioning whether it's worth it, believe me, it is. Everyone who sees it will understand that you and this team are for real. That after ten years, you're not fading—you're just getting warmed up."

He turns it over. "What cut of merchandise?"

I square my shoulders. "Twenty percent."

"Five."

"Twelve."

He turns it over. "Fine. Have the revised contract to my assistant before I change my mind."

I turn toward the door, hiding my grin until I have a hand on the cherry wood, when his voice reaches me.

"And Nova?"

"Yes?" I glance back to find him studying me as though he's never seen me before.

"This wall better be fucking spectacular."

~

CLAY

Nova: I did it.

The message comes when I'm getting off the plane after the road game.

It was a win, which puts everyone in a good mood.

But Nova's words are what make me smile.

Clay: Yeah you did.

The next day, I go in for a meeting with the coaches to watch game tape. On the way out of the meeting, I head by her wall and find her there.

She's wearing leggings and a long-sleeved shirt that rises up her back when she stretches, her hair pulled back in a pink ponytail.

The feeling washing over me isn't only desire, but pride. I'm fucking proud of her and I want to tell her.

"What are you painting now?" Jay asks.

She pulls off her headphones. "The team. Miles, Rookie, Atlas, Clay, you."

He folds his arms. "You're gonna make me bigger, right?"

"You're already three times life size," I drawl.

Rookie dissolves into laughter, and Jay hits me in the arm. He still clears six feet, but he's the shortest of all of us.

"We should celebrate," I say, and her eyes warm on mine.

"Yeah, it was a good win." Miles thinks I'm talking about that.

"I think I'm going to go home. Maybe take a bath." She stretches, her eyes closing as her hands lift overhead.

"I could give you a massage," Miles offers.

She laughs. "That's a great offer. Raincheck."

"We're going to Mile High," Rookie says.

Nova's gaze goes to me, as if she's gauging my reaction.

I look between the guys. "I'm gonna pass."

Rookie's got my back, and with only a little needling, they continue without me.

"Your game was good," she says when it's the two of us alone in the massive hallway.

"Not as good as yours. What'd you get?"

"Twelve percent." Her face screws up. "I asked for twenty. He countered at five."

"That's my girl." The words are out before I think, but her eyes brighten. "Let me drive you home," I say.

She collects her jacket, and we head for the parking garage side by side.

As we get into the car, I clear my throat, preparing to say what I practiced on the plane.

"I know you said you needed time to think, but I've been thinking too. The night of the wedding, there were a few things going on."

She straightens in her seat but doesn't look at me.

"But the most important one was that I cared about you, and instead of seeing that through, I panicked."

"I forgive you."

"You do?" I echo, wary.

"Yes. We can be friends."

Her words are like an axe to my damned chest as I pull into the parking garage and into my spot. "I don't want to be your friend."

She leans an elbow against the window frame and peers back at me, smiling. "You want me to text you naked pics?"

The fuck is she playing at?

I'll go along with it for now. "Yeah. That'd be good."

"Okay, then."

I cut the engine and lean my head back against the seat as she lets her words sink in.

"There's obviously still a connection between us," Nova goes on while I'm still speechless. "If we focus on the physical, I think it would keep things simple. Protect everyone," she goes on in a rush.

Well, fuck.

Now I'm the one on my heels.

With any other woman any other time, I'd be relieved she wants to keep boundaries clear.

But with Nova, it bothers me.

When I said I wanted her, I meant all of her.

Is it even possible to draw a line through this woman that separates her heart from the rest of her?

Why the hell would anyone try?

We get out of the car and walk in silence to the elevator. I wait for her to go first, holding the door.

She hits the button for her floor, and I hit mine.

I frown at her the whole way up, wishing to hell I could see what's going on inside her pretty head.

"You don't have to do this," I start.

"I'm doing exactly what I want to do," she counters.

When the doors slide open at her floor, I follow her out.

She stops at her door and turns back to me. Her tongue darts out to lick her lips. "I don't know if you know this, but Brooke has an insanely big jacuzzi bath."

Nova unlocks the door and tugs her ponytail holder out with her free hand.

My throat dries.

Dammit.

I'm no saint. I don't even play one for the cameras.

I try to summon every ounce of restraint in my body to remind us both that there are more important things than sex.

Inside, she hangs up her jacket and holds out a hand for mine. I pass it over.

"Is Brooke here?" It's more cough than words.

"No, she's at an event tonight."

Nova reaches for the hem of her shirt and drags it up over her head, revealing a pink lace bra a few shades lighter than her hair. Her tits are curved and tempting.

A few days ago, I would've been thrilled with

this Nova. Now, I'm wondering if our talk gave her the wrong idea. I don't want her in bed at the expense of her heart.

I want all of her.

I follow her down the hall, kicking off my shoes. My T-shirt goes next, along with her leggings and underwear and bra. I can't swallow my groan as her body is revealed in all its glory.

I drag her against me, my mouth crushing hers.

Goddamn, she feels perfect. I've dreamed about her like this so many times.

"You're so warm," she mumbles against my lips.

"Gonna make you warm too," I promise.

Without breaking our kiss, I reach past her to turn on the jacuzzi. She puts the plug in the tub and steps inside, tugging me after her.

I resist. The idea of following her in and taking her in the water, hearing her moans echo off the tile, is sweet heaven. But I want to spoil her.

"You got any girly stuff?"

She blinks at me. "What, like tampons?" Nova's laughter fills the air, and I'm suddenly awkward as a teenager.

"Nah. Like..." I struggle to think of the word. "Bath stuff."

"Oh. Under the sink."

I go looking for anything in pastel colors and find some smelly epsom salts under the sink. I pour them in the water, then I shift onto the tile at the edge of the sunken tub behind her shoulders.

"What are you doing?"

"Giving you a massage."

"You could do it in the tub."

No, I can't.

When I start touching her in the jacuzzi, feeling her slippery curves, it'll be that much harder to hold back.

Desire got the better of me last time. She's giving me another chance, even if she wouldn't call it that, and the hardest part will be winning her heart.

I'm committed. This is the most important game I've ever played, and nothing's getting in the way of my victory.

It'll be like rehabbing my knee.

Slow and steady.

One step at a time.

My fingers start at the base of her neck, pressing in deep. I work my way down her back, taking my time and kneading out knots as I go. Her skin is soft and warm under my touch, and she moans softly.

"Too hard?" I ask.

"No. You're really good at that."

My cock twitches, and I tell it to calm the fuck down.

I focus on her, rubbing tiny circles with fingers that are huge against her delicate muscles and bones. I press my thumbs into the small of her back and work my way up to her shoulders. She sighs in pleasure, tilting her head back until it rests against me.

"How're things with your sister?" I ask.

Nova frowns. "You want to talk about Mari right now?"

No, but I want to know how Nova's life is going and her sister is part of that.

"Okay. Things are better than they were when I got here." She fills me in, ending on, "Except...it was Mari who set me up on that date."

Course it was.

My shoulders tense. "Want me to tell her to stop?"

Nova laughs softly. "I let her know I wasn't looking to date right now."

Satisfaction reverberates through my body, until I realize maybe that policy extends to me.

"How was the road game?" she asks under her breath.

"Tough," I admit. "But no back-to-backs this week at least."

I move my hands to her arms, kneading in slow circles. My fingertips find their way along the length of her neck, trailing feather-light touches that induce a shiver from head to toe before settling into a steady rhythm at the base of her skull that has her sighing with delight.

With each stroke, Nova relaxes more and more.

"Get in. Please," she sighs.

"Why?"

"I want to give *you* a massage," she says, her voice dragging along my spine with wicked precision. "The kind you can't get anywhere else."

"I can get any kind I want," I tease.

She turns to face me, her eyes narrowing. "You better not."

"You jealous, Pink?" I'm strangely into it, not because I want her to question that she's the only woman I think about that way, but because it means she cares.

Nova lifts one shoulder in a shrug.

"Last chance to get in," she murmurs. "Are you really saying no?"

I'm fighting the urge to climb in with her, to strip off the last of my clothes and fuck her tight pussy until she's begging me to let her come the way she's begging me to join her now.

What she means is, can I fuck her and not care about her? Not need her and not need her to need me back?

"No. I mean, yeah, I'm saying no."

As much as I want this, I won't take it until she admits she wants to give us another chance.

She sighs and slumps back against my chest.

"That a dealbreaker?" I murmur against her cheek. "You going to kick me out if I won't be your fuckboy?"

"I suppose not." She holds out a hand for a towel. "Let's watch a movie."

We settle on *Pretty Woman*. Nova likes rom-coms and Julia Roberts, and tonight I want to give her what she wants.

We're curled up on the couch together as we watch the business man getting stripped down by the crass, charming sex worker. Nova let me pull her into my lap, a softer version of our position in the tub because we're both dressed, even if she's only in little shorts and a T-shirt.

I'm a breath away from looking up whether blue balls can cause permanent damage.

"I appreciate what you did for me with James," she murmurs as we watch. "My entire life I've had reasons not to believe in myself. You believe in me as if it's a given. That means more than I can express." She hums. "When it comes to you, I need to trust you, but I also need time to know I can trust my own judgment. Does that make sense?"

"Sort of?" I've questioned other people lots but rarely myself.

In her position, though, with what she's been through growing up and her parents' deaths and dating manipulative assholes, I can see how she'd second-guess.

"I get why they don't kiss," she goes on, still watching the TV. "It's easier to keep things impersonal."

"Impersonal" my ass.

"Are you laughing?" she goes on, twisting to look up at me.

"A little."

"Why?"

"Because that ship sailed before I took you to Red Rocks that first night," I murmur.

She sighs against me. "It was so exciting being around you. You were larger than life, but you made me feel special. I still remember that 'crunchy peanut butter' line."

"Wasn't a line. I wanted you to know me."

"I thought I did know you."

I shift up on my elbow to get a better look at her. "You do. You fucking do, Nova." It matters that she believes it.

She shifts her body and turns into me, her breasts brushing my chest. Her eyes find mine, the bright blue pierced by dark pupils.

"I keep thinking about the other night in the back room at Mile High," she murmurs. "It all happened so fast."

Whatever Richard Gere is doing with the out-of-his-league sex worker is forgotten. There's no world outside of the heat rising on this couch.

Just like I couldn't keep my feelings for Nova out of the desire I felt earlier, now a carnal hunger bleeds into the edges of my emotions.

She smells like some kind of wildflower, and I want to suck all the honey out of her.

My body is already tense from the feel of her,

but now my abs clench and my cock throbs. "We can slow it down next time."

Her face tips up. "Really?"

I've got her attention now. "Uh-huh. Tell me what you liked about it."

Her eyes are big and round, her lips parting. She can definitely feel how turned on I am, and she's into it. "I liked your mouth on me."

No shit.

"What else?"

"I liked watching you stroke yourself. I liked seeing you get off."

Desire jolts down my spine.

This is dangerous territory, and not what I planned.

But I told her we had to talk, that I wanted her to open up to me, and that's what we're doing, right?

I skim her hip with my palm. Her legs are smooth and soft, and I hitch her knee over my thigh.

"Just the thought of you gets me off," I murmur. "I'm that hot for you, Pink."

My fingers slide up the inside of her shorts.

Damn.

She's hot and slippery, her skin like satin fire against me.

"You're so fucking wet," I tell her.

Her eyes darken with desire.

I'm between her legs, pushing in just far enough to make her gasp. The sensations are too much, and she grips my shoulders to stay upright.

"That feels... incredible."

"Good," I whisper back.

I play with her, enjoying every second of her arousal. The heat between us is palpable, and I lean in to kiss her, but she turns her face at the last second.

I capture her chin and turn her back to me.

"This isn't make-believe, Nova. You want me to fuck you, you're damn well going to feel it. If you decide after that you're not willing to take a chance on us, that's one thing. But I'm gonna hold your eyes wide open and show you everything we are first."

13

CLAY

My tongue pushes into her mouth as I grip her hips with both hands.

She moans softly against my lips, a sound that drives me wild. My body aches for hers as I press against her, our tongues dancing in perfect synchronization as we get lost in each other.

All I want is to be inside her. But instead of giving in to impulse here, I get off the couch and lift her, her legs wrapping around my hips as I carry her down the hall towards the bedrooms.

"First one is me," she murmurs.

I turn where she says and tear my gaze from her long enough to look around.

The room itself is soft pink, the queen mattress

covered in a white bedspread. There's a desk covered in art supplies and a sketchpad.

I'm curious what she's working on, but I've got my hands full.

I cross the room and lay her gently on the bed. Her hair spreads out on the pillow, and she looks like a goddess or a fairy or both.

I take my time undressing her, feeling her eyes on me the entire time.

"You're so fucking beautiful," I say.

She smiles as she reaches for me, her hands stroking my chest, my arms, my abs.

I yank off my pants, tossing them off the side of the bed without taking my eyes from her.

We're skin to skin, my body tense and my cock already a steel rod between us.

"I've thought about this a million times," I tell her.

Her lips curve. "Sounds like an exaggeration."

"It's a conservative estimate."

I press two fingers inside her, and she arches up to meet me.

Her body is so hot, her pussy squeezing my fingers.

She's not wrong to think it'll be a tight fit.

I'm six-five and have a cock to match.

It's my job to make her ready.

As ready as she can be.

When she reaches for my cock, I gently press her hand against the bedspread.

"Let me."

She bites her lip and allows me to explore her. Tonight, there's no one barging in. There's nothing stopping us.

My fingers work inside her, playing with her clit and her pussy until she tightens around me.

"Oh, God. Clay. Yes..."

She's slick and turned on, making little sounds even as I withdraw from her.

I shift off the bed to grab a condom from my wallet. When I come back, she's panting and staring up at me from her elbows.

But her attention falls to my cock.

"You want this, sweetheart?"

She smiles, breathless. "Yes."

Adrenaline surges through me as I nudge her back down. "Wider. Need those ankles spread, gorgeous."

She hesitates. I reach for her chin and tilt it up so her eyes meet mine.

"I said I'd go slow. I meant it." My lips brush hers.

She wraps her legs around my hips again, and I adjust her. Her ass fills my hands, and I can't wait to be deep inside her.

"Clay?" she whispers, her fingers threading into my hair.

"Yeah?"

She bites her lip, looking unsure.

I brush my mouth across hers softly. "Do you trust me?"

"Yes."

I press inside her, an inch at a time.

Fuck.

Oh, sweet fuck.

She feels so damn good.

Slow's gonna be harder than I thought.

Her ribs expand, her eyes widening.

I channel all the patience I have as I adjust her in my arms, and when she relaxes, I rock back in.

Her breathing is shallow.

After a few small movements, I see it.

Her pupils dilate, her eyes softening.

"Yeah, sweetheart. That's it."

Her head falls back. Whether it's from her body responding to my patient insistence or from my words of praise, I'm not sure. So, I continue both.

"You're so good."

The next time, I slide an inch deeper. My fingers dig into her ass, my teeth grinding together. She sighs in relief, and that exhale has her relaxing.

"Clay!" she gasps as I sink all the way inside her.

I shift onto my back and seat her on top.

She lifts off, cringing a little.

Is she hating this?

The thought devastates me.

But she lowers herself back down, one experimental inch at a time.

My hands settle on her thighs, and I force myself not to hurry her. Her eyes drift down my body, all the way to where we're joined.

"You really are massive everywhere." She says it breathlessly, with a hint of accusation.

"Never apologized for that before, but if you want me to, I will."

"Maybe." But her lips twitch too.

Damn if this girl isn't everything good in the world.

"We can stop," I grunt, even though it kills me to say it.

"You wouldn't be mad?"

"No, I won't be mad." I might die of sexual frustration, but I'd do that before I'd hurt her again.

She tightens around me, and my smile evaporates.

My abs flex hard, my thighs clenching. I'm not used to letting someone fuck me.

I'd let her do anything she wanted.

Carve her name into my skin with her nails, red against the black tattoos covering me.

I move my feet up the bed to support her, but she seems fascinated by what we're doing together.

"Oh!" She swallows, her head tipping back. "Ohhhhh."

"What is it?" I murmur.

"I like watching you. Watching us," she whispers.

And a whole other ream of ideas comes tumbling through my brain at her saying that.

Mirrors.

Photos.

Videos.

I get even harder.

"How does it feel for you?" she asks.

"Like heaven and hell all at once," I say honestly.

"Hell?" Nova cocks her head, her lips curving. They're a shade darker than her hair.

Yeah, because you're in control, and I'd give you all of it.

She rocks over me, gaining confidence.

"Tell me how you feel," I say under my breath.

"It feels wrong. Like we shouldn't be doing this." She arches her hips on a moan. "But somehow, that only makes me want to do it more."

I fucking growl.

"Ride me," I urge.

She lifts her hips a few inches, then slowly slides back down.

I've never been religious, but I'd worship at her temple every day for the rest of my life for a moment of this.

My jaw clenches, and my fingers dig hard into her hips and ass.

Nova repeats the movement, a little longer, a little deeper.

I change the angle, helping hit new places.

"That's it." My lips brush her ear, the soft skin of her cheek.

Nova's hair sticks to her neck as her hips move faster in time with the deepening of my thrusts.

So.

Fucking.

Sexy.

Her body is kissed with sweat from the effort, and I give her a moment to adjust before pulling back, then sinking back in.

"Take all of me," I groan. "Every fucking inch is for you."

We move together, building up momentum.

She moans louder as I thrust harder and faster. Her grip on me tightens, her fingers and her pussy.

Her hips are rolling too, grinding to meet mine.

I'm so deep in her I swear I can feel her heartbeat through my cock.

I'm doing everything in my power to rock her world.

From the moment she looked up at me on the couch, it was a given she was going to rock mine.

"Oh God. I'm close," she moans.

I want her to finish first. Not only because it's the right thing to do, but because I want to watch her lose control.

"Come on my cock, baby. Let me feel you come undone."

I shove myself up onto my elbows, taking her breast in my mouth and sucking hard.

She twists and grinds on me, her body clenching as she cries out.

When she comes, it's sweaty and real. I want to imprint every moan, every flutter, every arching curve on my memory forever.

My release is intense, an explosion of pleasure starting at the base of my spine.

Stars.

All I see is fucking stars, and *her*, and if there's a heaven, it's this moment right here.

I fall back, and she collapses onto me.

The thudding behind my ribs matches hers. Our skin sticks together, her floral scent settling over me like a blanket I want to wrap around me.

"You were right," she murmurs. "That wasn't so bad."

I shift up on my elbows to stare down at her. "Not so bad?!"

Nova's lips curve, her eyes dancing with humor and satisfaction. "Okay, it was really good. You're so sexy, with or without clothes. This is just one more way to have fun together."

The pleasure from her words hits in a different way than the orgasm. I love how honest she is with me.

"You're the sexy one," I murmur, brushing her

hair from her face. "Thought I might die if you tapped out early."

She grins. "I'm guessing there are other ways to finish you off."

"Uh-huh. You keep talking like that, I'll show you. Sooner than later."

I slip out from under her long enough to dispose of the condom, then return, tugging her over me again. I'm stroking her hair when her words cut into my thoughts.

"You don't seem like the kind of guy who panics."

"Hmm?"

"What you said before. About panicking and that's why you gave me that letter? You don't seem like a guy who panics."

"I do panic. I don't show it." I rarely explain myself unless it's at media going over my game, but this is Nova. I want to let her in, so I reach for the words to express the things I normally try to keep hidden. "It turns over and over inside me, getting worse and worse. I bury it, like throwing dirt on lava, but eventually the dirt gets burned up too."

"How do you fix it?" Her hand strokes my face, her eyes full of compassion.

"I don't. I guess I got used to feeling terrible

and not showing it. When it came to you..." I swallow as the deal rises up in my mind. Mentioning it feels crass and ugly after what we just did. "I didn't want to fuck up the things you've worked for. I knew I'd hate myself if I did that. I guess I've never trusted myself outside of basketball."

"Then it's definitely time to start."

I pull her into my arms and lock them around her from behind, getting comfortable.

"I'm not letting you leave again," I murmur.

She's already asleep.

14

NOVA

"*N*ova?"

Brooke's voice from the other room has me blinking open my eyes.

I was in the middle of a wild dream. One where I was flying and falling and aroused all at once. I inhale deeply, my ribs pressing against a hard, warm band of muscle and bone that smells deliciously male.

It was only a dream, except...

There's a wide, firm chest pressed against my back. The possessive arm around my waist is carved with black lines, bold swirls that look like ropes surrounding not only him but me too.

Clay stayed over.

I wanted to hold him at a distance. It worked,

until he carried me into my bedroom and proceeded to strip away every idea I've ever had about sex.

It was the closest I've ever felt to another human and not only because I'm deliciously sore in places I've never been sore before.

The first time was intense enough. But when I woke a few hours later, he was right there ready to go again.

And again.

Now, a hard shape presses against my butt, and I sneak a look over my shoulder.

Oh God. His cock looks every bit as huge today as he felt last night, thick and long and hard.

When he started to sink inside me, I thought it was a mistake. Like he might tear me in half and I would be the stupid girl who thought this was physically possible despite obvious visual clues to the contrary.

I can't decide if I deserve a medal for taking him or if he deserves one for, I don't know... just being Clay Wade?!

"Nova!" Brooke calls again. "Are you awake? I need to ask you something important!"

I try to free myself from the arm, but it only bands tighter. Clay mutters against my neck, his monster dick growing more insistent against my ass.

"Let me go, you brute," I mutter.

"Never."

My heart skips, and my grip on his arm loosens for a moment.

When I relax, he does too, and I catch him in a moment of weakness and dive out of bed. Tucking a robe from my closet around me, I turn back to see him watching me through dark slits of eyes.

"Morning, Pink."

Damn if he doesn't look sexy as hell naked in my bed, like every dream I've ever had only better.

"Brooke's home. Don't come out until I say so," I warn.

He flips a palm, noncommittal.

I glare as I let myself out, pulling the door closed behind me.

My roommate is in the kitchen, making eggs.

"What was the question?" My voice comes out raspy. I clear my throat.

"Christmas. The guys are playing Christmas Day, but we always have dinner together after. You should join."

I bite my lip. "Mari texted me about it

yesterday and invited me to spend Christmas with her and Harlan."

"We'll do the entire family." Before I can answer, Brooke's gaze cuts over my shoulder. "Morning, Clay."

"Morning." I turn to find him wearing sweatpants and nothing else.

He looks like some Marvel-movie god, his muscles rippling under the tattoos. He takes up half the living room.

"Great flowers you sent last week," Brooke offers. "Five stars."

"Glad you like them. Wasn't sure Nova did." He drops into a chair at the table.

My mouth works for a moment before I can produce sound. "Um. Clay was just—"

"Sneaking out the morning after."

"That's not it," I start.

Brooke crosses to the coffee table and grabs the wad of fabric off it, tossing it at Clay. He catches it. He starts to tug the shirt on but, at my perusal, thinks better of it.

His wink when he catches me looking makes me want to die.

Oh my God. I wish for the days before I hooked

up with a hot athlete and my body took over my brain.

"I'm sure you have questions," I say to my roommate, trying to be mature about this.

"Not really. I know you guys split, but as long as it's consensual, I get it. Girl's gotta get hers. He's convenient," Brooke offers.

"I'm not convenient." Clay frowns.

"He's so inconvenient," I add.

For my heart and my life and my future.

But I'm stronger than I was, and this time I can manage my own heart.

"You want coffee?" Brooke asks.

"Sure. Thanks."

"He's not staying."

They ignore me.

"I'm glad you kids had fun last night," Brooke says easily.

"Girl tired me out. I never sleep this late."

I'm a little pleased by his assessment, forgetting he shouldn't still be here when Brooke sets a coffee in front of him.

"You remembered how I like it," he says.

"Miles told me."

"You pay a lot of attention to what he says, huh?"

Brooke tosses him a look. "Watch it, or I'll dump that over your head."

Clay turns back to me. "It's not a hookup."

"It's not?" Brooke and I echo.

"Nah." Clay studies me over his coffee. "It's serious."

What the hell?

"Really?" Brooke lifts both brows smugly. "I love that for you."

"Excuse us, B."

I lunge for his wrist, intending to drag Clay to the bedroom or the bathroom or maybe just the front door so he can stop messing with my head and my life.

Before I can, Brooke holds up both hands. "I'll give you guys a second." She takes her coffee and shoots me a grin before heading toward the balcony.

"Where'd you get that idea?" I demand when she's gone, the door closed behind her. "And could you please put on that shirt?"

"It's dirty." Clay rests an elbow on the back of the next chair, drinking his coffee as if we're in his place, not mine.

"You like dirty."

His slow grin is feral. "So do you."

Good girl.

Come on my cock, baby. Let me feel you come undone.

I flush. I'm getting distracted from what's important.

"What was that about? The serious thing?"

"You're mine. It's obvious every second I'm touching you."

"Wow, the arrogance never quits."

"It's the truth. I know it, and if it takes you a second to catch up because you need to trust me again or for some other reason, I'll wait."

My heart skips.

Last night, I figured he'd be thrilled with my proposal to keep things physical. His stubborn commitment to the idea of more was not in the plan.

"I believe you think you want that," I say, "but really, you like pissing a circle around me and telling any other guys they can't come near."

"That's not it." His eyes dial up in intensity. "I want to talk like we used to. I want to take you out. Things click for me when I'm around you, and I think they do for you too."

His words make me swallow. "I'm building my own life, my own independence."

"I don't want to take that from you. I liked you from the moment I met you. I like you even more now."

Clay's expression softens, and I feel myself weakening.

He shifts forward. "Come here."

"Why?"

"Because we're not going to negotiate our relationship on opposite sides of the room."

Reluctantly, I step closer. He pulls me into his lap.

That's not what we're doing. But when I feel his warmth, I'm not so sure.

I want to trust him, but this time, I can't be stupid about it.

"I don't want anyone to know," I say.

He shrugs a shoulder. "Brooke already knows. Plus a few guys on the team."

"The team?!" My brows shoot up. "Well, I don't want Mari or Harlan to know. Not yet." Not because I'm ashamed, but because I'd have to admit to my sister exactly how things started with me and Clay and how distracted I was during the days and weeks leading up to her wedding.

I expect him to argue, but he looks relieved. "The guys will keep quiet. And it's better if Harlan and James think I'm entirely focused on basketball."

"Because you're still planning on making the jump to LA."

"Eventually. It's taking longer than I figured."

I try not to think too hard about that. When I first met him, Mari's wedding was our expiry date. This new one looming over us is messier because neither of us knows when it might come.

Somehow, it makes me bolder.

"If we do this, I want to be exclusive," I say.

Clay brushes the hair from my face, stroking his thumb down my cheek. "So, no more Kodashians?"

I shake my head, and he laughs.

"What's so funny?" I demand.

"I haven't touched another woman since I laid eyes on you, Pink."

Well, damn. Didn't expect that to feel as good as it does.

"Okay, then. So, in public, we're discreet," I say.

"In private, you're mine."

Something about the way he says it makes me want to plaster my body to his and let him do whatever he wants with me.

He lifts my chin with a finger. "You like sneaking around with me. It makes you hot." He brushes his lips over mine.

"That's not true," I protest weakly.

"I feel you getting wet." His hand grinds against my pussy through my pajama bottoms, and my eyes drift closed.

His mouth and touch are destroying me, making every part of my body light up with pleasure.

I've almost forgotten we're in the dining room, my roommate a few feet away outside.

The slider door opens. "You two make up?"

"Yup," Clay says at the same time I say, "For now."

"Good. So, about Christmas?" Brooke asks again.

Clay drags me against him, wrapping his arms around me. "We'll be there."

15

CLAY

*B*asketball Christmas isn't like normal Christmas.

The top teams play games on the day, then after we celebrate with our families.

I never really got the magic of it before this year, when I wake up in my own bed, Nova curled next to me.

"Merry Christmas," I murmur in her ear, stroking her hair.

She huffs a breath but doesn't move.

Damn, she's gorgeous. Her hair is dark blond at the roots and pink at the tips, like some wild fairy's. I want to see her bright blue eyes blink up at me, wake her with my hands and lips, but I should let her sleep.

She's been working late all week on the next section of her mural. Her talent is almost as impressive as her dedication.

I've been busy too.

The Kodiaks are sitting third in the Western Conference, surprising all the sportscasters and the oddsmakers.

Rookie is getting his shit together and has strung together some good solo performances, Miles is hitting every three-pointer he tries, and Jay's held us together. My knee is as good as it's been in months.

Yeah, we've had a lighter schedule for the past couple of weeks, with an extended homestand that wraps up today, but I know to take wins when we can get them and not question it.

I've never had someone in my life since I turned pro, but I can't get enough of Nova. We don't get as much time together as I want, but every second makes me crave her more.

I'm counting the firsts with her.

First time she slept over: last week.

First time I showed her pics of my family: this weekend.

First time I made her laugh so hard she cried: yesterday.

The other day, she told me she couldn't come over because she was working, so I brought her dinner and made her sit down for twenty minutes so we could eat together.

The way she looked up at me with those big, blue eyes like I was the best thing to happen to her all day...

Fuck, a man could get used to that.

Every time she says my name, I'm a little less mine and a little more hers.

We've kept things effectively on the DL. No one's mentioned the possessive way I look at her, how she smiles at me, the fact that I find any excuse to touch her.

Today will be another story, with all of us attending dinner with the team and Harlan. I still haven't figured out the best way to deal with that situation.

Until I do, I'm ignoring it.

My phone is already blowing up with holiday greetings as I force myself out of bed to start my routine.

Kat: Merry Christmas, loser. I'll try to watch the game.

I hit her contact.

"Wow, a call and everything?" she drawls.

"Merry Christmas, shrimp. Surprised you were up so early."

"Andy was opening presents hours ago, like any self-respecting nine-year-old."

Kat's boyfriend has a couple years on me, and as much as that irritates me, he's a decent guy. He's raising a kid on his own after his wife died tragically, and I respect the way he looks out for his family. He also loves the hell out of Kat.

I miss my sister. She's in grad school out east, and I'm here and everywhere. When we play in New York, I send tickets for her and, for the past year, for Daniel and Andy too.

"What else are you doing?" I ask.

"Mmm, nothing special. I'll fill you in later."

"Did you get the gifts I sent?" Matching designer sweaters for her and Daniel, plus a fun-sized basketball net with a bunch of limited-edition swag for the kid.

"I don't think so."

"It says it was delivered yesterday."

"Oh." Her voice sounds weird. "I gotta go, Clay. Merry Christmas."

I say it back, and we click off.

"Merry Christmas. Happy Hanukkah. Best wishes to you and your family and everything you celebrate." Miles dances around the court at shootaround, setting elf hats on heads.

He ends on Coach, who glares but holds out a hand.

"Less antics, more shooting," Coach gripes.

"Why're you so tense?" I demand.

"Nothing. Management and owners are at it again," he amends at last, his voice low enough only I can hear.

He means Harlan and James.

I catch a stray ball and square to the basket, letting off a shot that swishes through the net.

"What are they fighting about?" I can't resist asking. "The team is winning."

"Harlan wants a deep run in the playoffs and is talking about trading a few pieces to set us up for the postseason. But Parker wants to double down on the winning now because he likes seeing his name in the news."

The next ball comes to me, and I fire it on to Rookie to shoot.

"So, what's the problem? Let them fight it out."

"Problem is I get stuck in the middle like wadded up underwear." He flashes teeth before turning to the other guys.

Coach is the only one in a bad mood. As fans flood the building, collecting the special "Beary Christmas" T-shirts Chloe had made for the thousands of spectators, there's a decidedly celebratory vibe.

Jay nudges me. "If we win today, we'll have as many wins as Vegas thought we'd have through all-star break."

I know we've been beating expectations, but I try to tune out the noise like oddsmakers. Still, this is momentous.

But the antics don't seem to hurt us. Everyone is in a festive spirit, the fans flowing into the seats singing carols that fill the stadium.

From the opening tip-off, we're dialed in. Our opponents are too, and all of us throw everything we have into the game. It's playoff-like energy against a strong Boston team, and we scrap the entire way.

During a timeout, we're catching our breath when I see Miles looking up at the stands.

Halfway up the first section are Brooke and Nova and Mari.

It's good to see my girl in the stands. I like knowing she's there while I do what I was put on this earth to do.

All the way through the end of the second quarter, I focus on the fact that my girl is here.

I play my mind out.

The crowd hollers and swells, and anytime I look up to see her, she's on her feet.

"Go, Clay!"

The voice hollers at halftime when we're heading back to the locker room via the tunnel, and I look up into the crowd and see Kat and Daniel and Andy.

Andy bounces on his feet as he sees me noticing. Kat waves, and I grin.

Sneaky sister.

I didn't expect her to surprise me like this.

Looking between her and Nova and my guys, I can't remember the last time I was this happy, on the court or off it.

In the second half, we're even more dominant than in the first.

There are some tricky spots, but we couldn't play any better.

When I look back up toward Nova, she's smiling at me. I give it right back to her before I realize it's not only the girls in those seats this time.

Harlan's next to them, watching me steadily.

I shove down the discomfort and concentrate back on the huddle.

We get the win, and the building erupts in red and green and gold streamers. They don't go with the Kodiaks' purple, but no one cares.

NOVA

"Get in!" Mari nods toward the passenger side of the car as we bounce into the parking garage after the game. "Harlan will meet us at home."

Today might be a holiday, but there's a lot at stake.

I haven't had Christmas with my sister in a few years, plus Harlan and the entire team are involved.

Including the guy I'm secretly dating.

But no big deal.

I eye the back seat filled with wrapped gifts, but I squeeze into the passenger seat. "That was an incredible game. You a fan yet?"

"It's growing on me," she admits. "It helps that the team is having a good season."

"Harlan relaxing a few notches?"

"Never." She grins as she backs out of the spot.

I'm grateful we're in the team section because it's easier to get out. The garage is full of honking people wishing one another well.

Mari cuts me a look as she waits for the gate to rise so we can turn onto the street. "Thank you for being so excited about the team. I get that sports aren't your thing."

"It's the family business now," I counter.

"Well, I'm proud of you for doing the art. Harlan said it's going to be incredible."

The drive is easy, tiny flecks of snow making it feel extra festive.

My mural is growing and evolving every day.

So are things between me and Clay.

When he's in Denver, he's attentive, but the sport is grueling for the players. I have new appreciation as I see it up close. All the ice baths and massages and physio in the world can't fix the toll it takes on the human body.

He's opening up more to me. He lives in his head, but I feel as if I have a pass to peek inside.

Maybe not an all-access pass, but I don't think he's ever given one.

And as for the secrecy, I honestly like that we're privately an item.

He's a magnet for attention, good and bad. Being with him means getting swept into the same storm.

I'm still figuring out how to navigate my own life, not to mention his.

The winning streak for the team is a plus. But every time I check the standings, I'm reminded LA is even higher.

Clay's dream.

His destination.

His legacy.

He watches every one of their games, studying the players and the schemes.

I don't know what that means for him or for us, but I try to enjoy what we have and not think too hard about it.

When we arrive at Harlan's house, a huge catering truck is out front.

"You weren't going to cook for thirty?" I tease.

"Do you remember when we tried to cook for ten at the trailer? We nearly burned it down."

I help her carry the presents inside, laughing the entire time.

An hour later, Mari and I have changed outfits. She's wearing a cozy white cashmere sweater, and I'm in a black dress and tights. We've fluffed the place and put all the gifts under the huge tree.

"We're heeeere!" Chloe is the first to arrive, bursting in the door with Jay and Brooke in tow.

I'm stunned to see the elegant head of PR wearing dangly red bulb earrings plus an antler headband and a sweater with a Kodiaks bear twisted up in a strand of lights.

Mari stares too. "Who are you, and what have you done with Chloe?"

"Let me be the first to tell you," Jay says solemnly, "this woman is a Christmas fiend. Every year she's body-snatched by a giant elf and doesn't return until New Year's."

Coming in the door after are Rookie and Miles with Waffles in his arms. When he sets the Frenchie down, I get a good look at his knitted black and gold sweater with H's emblazoned on every inch.

Chloe slaps two bottles of red wine against Jay's chest. "Kitchen. Holiday sangria. Now."

Jay straightens to his full height—he's shorter than the other guys but still plenty tall to look down at his ex with amusement.

"You're not the boss of me, elf. We're not dating."

She smiles sweetly. "No, but I remember where your balls are, and my nails will be in them in five seconds if you don't follow orders."

He lifts both bottles in a sign of grudging surrender, then steps out of his boots and crosses to the other room.

"I'm turning on the game," Rookie says, heading for the big-screen TV in the living room.

I frown. "I thought the game is over."

"The LA game," chorus Jay from the kitchen, Chloe from the dining room, and Harlan, Rookie, and Miles in here.

Coach and Harlan are in the door next.

Everyone's here except for Clay.

My phone buzzes.

Grumpy Baller: Hey, can you ask Mari if there's room for three more?

Surprise hits me.

I didn't talk to him after the game except to send a text saying congrats. I knew he'd be here when he got through his post-routine and media, but now I'm wondering what's up.

I go to the kitchen. "Hey, Mar? Clay's asking if he can bring three people."

"Sure."

I'm halfway out the door when she calls after me. "Wait, why did he ask you?"

My heart kicks in my chest.

Because we talk every day. Most nights, I fall asleep in his arms. In the morning, I wake up to his heavy breathing. I'm totally falling for him, and I can't help it.

I shrug. "Maybe no one else was answering their phones."

I text him back and grab a drink before joining the others in the living room, where they're half watching the television and talking.

When Clay arrives, the girl at his side makes my mouth fall open.

She's familiar from pictures he has at his place.

There's a cute kid around ten next to her and a handsome guy hovering over her shoulder.

"Everyone, this is my sister, Kat. Kat, this is everyone," Clay says.

"Nova," Kat says, cocking her head at me. "It's great to finally meet you."

Finally? She throws her arms around me, and I cut a look at Clay, but he's tight-lipped.

They grab drinks, and we set the table as we wait for the others. Gradually, everyone trickles in —Atlas, the bench players, Harlan...

"You're late!" Rookie calls. "You guys are missing the last quarter of the LA game."

Clay and I exchange a look.

"I'm not missing anything," he says with a wink.

Dinner feels as if we're all one big family. One with tension and issues, sure, but today everyone sets it aside. There's gossiping about sports and family and friends, and even Waffles gets his own special meal.

We go around the table saying things were thankful for.

Harlan says, "Family."

Chloe says, "A day away from the news cycle."

Clay says, "Second chances," with a stealth look at me.

Spending today with Clay has me imagining what it would be like to spend more holidays with him.

After dinner, we do a gift swap. Rather than having each person buy everyone a present, we set a value limit for each person to contribute a single gift to stick under the tree.

"I'm sorry, we didn't bring gifts," Kat says.

"I'll sit out, and Andy can play," Clay offers.

"Everyone, relax. I have extra," Mari insists.

In that moment, I'm grateful for her preparation.

I drew a number third from the start, and I'm drawn to a tiny box wrapped in pink.

I unwrap it to find a Louis Vuitton keychain in the shape of a bear.

"You might want to hang on to that," Clay suggests.

After the game, I'm heading into the kitchen carrying empty glasses when I hear Harlan's voice.

"I know what I saw."

Then Clay's voice. "Stay in your lane. You've got enough to worry about."

I don't know what's going on, but there are always Kodiaks tensions.

I'll ask him about it later. Not because I want to get in his business, but just in case he wants to vent.

At the end of the night, we head for the cars.

Clay insisted Kat, Andy, and Daniel stay at his place since he has an extra bedroom and a couch. When we all get back to our building, Clay pulls me aside in the parking garage.

"Come up tonight?" Clay asks.

"I'll come for breakfast. You haven't seen your sister in forever." I want to give them time to themselves.

He frowns but eventually nods. "Alright, but meet me for a few minutes tonight. I have something for you."

My mouth curves. "I have something for you too."

When we meet in the hall, Clay holds a huge wrapped gift.

Since we've only been dating a couple weeks, I wasn't sure about gift etiquette, but now I'm glad I got him something.

"What is this?" I demand.

"It goes with your other gift."

"Oh, wow. Mine isn't that impressive."

"I know you love a big package, Pink." His eyes glint as he takes the smaller one from me and unwraps it. "It's a book."

"A journal," I correct, pointing to the black swirls of ink across the tan surface. "I tried to replicate your tattoos on it because I thought it would be a safe space for you to write down all the things you don't tell the world. It would feel like home."

Clay's expression is unreadable as he turns the book over in his hands.

"It's cheesy," I say, laughing.

"No, I love it. Thank you." He pulls me up for a kiss I feel all the way to my toes. "Now your turn."

I unwrap the significantly larger package he passes me, and my jaw drops when I see the monogrammed LV fabric. "It's incredible," I gasp.

"It goes with the keychain. Figured you needed a new one. You got paint all over the other one."

"I can't believe you noticed."

"I notice everything when it comes to you." He says it in a rush of breath, distinctly un-Clay-like, and my attention lifts from the bag to him. "I've never wanted to know everything about anyone. But with you, I want to know what you love, what you hate. I want to see you at Christmas, like today, surrounded by your favorite people. It reminds me that this is what life is supposed to be like. What it can be like."

My chest is stretched tight, as if I inhaled each of his words and they're expanding inside me.

I glance back at the door.

"Come in for five minutes?" I whisper.

My fist is still clutched around the handle of the bag as Clay backs me into Brooke's apartment, his hand already grabbing my hip as his lips brush across mine.

"Make it ten."

16

NOVA

Nova: Thank you for dinner. How did you know I wouldn't have eaten?

Grumpy Baller: Call it a hunch.

*T*he week between Christmas and New Year's is quieter at the stadium and Clay has been playing two road games, so I take advantage to work on the wall.

He's started to check in with me if it's a long day, like he knows even without seeing that I'm perched on the ladder trying to create something worthy of this city, this team.

Tonight, it was nearly seven when I got home and took a bath.

When I got out, the was a message from the concierge to let me know dinner was waiting for me at the door.

The package contained tacos from my favorite Mexican place, plus fresh chips and salsa, as well as a six-pack of Gatorade with a note saying to "stay hydrated." More than enough food for me and Brooke, who came home soon after.

It was a seriously sweet gesture, especially considering Clay's first home game in over a week is tonight.

Grumpy Baller: You catch my game?

Nova: You were okay.

Grumpy Baller: "Okay" like you watched it with your hand in between your thighs?

Nova: Gasp.

Nova: I figured you'd want me to wait for you.

Grumpy Baller: Want you waiting in my bed.

Nova: Skip media or I'll start without you.

Flirting with Clay by text is becoming one of my favorite things.

It's even better when he's in Denver and waiting to see him is a matter of hours, not days.

We can't keep our hands off each other.

But because this is still new and his schedule is beyond demanding, it feels as if there's still so much we haven't done.

"UGHHHH!"

The shriek has my head snapping up from where I'm watching TV in the living room.

I'm off the couch the next second, padding down the hall and pushing wide the cracked door.

"Are you dead?" I ask as I scan my roommate's prone figure. She's sprawled like a ragdoll, her braids spilling across the duvet and her arms overhead.

"Emotionally," Brooke pants.

Since rooming together for the past couple of

months, we've gotten closer. We have our roomie routines, and I love our time together.

Now, Brooke tosses her phone on the bed. "I got this brand partnership and posted it. One of the girls from my sorority DMs me saying, 'So cute, I wish my brother could get me these kinds of gigs.'"

Her eyes squeeze shut.

I fold my arms. "You know that's bullshit. You deserve all your success."

"Obviously." She chews her lip. "But why do some girls have to tear others down? Like friends aren't really friends and it's just a label you slap on people in your social feed through college and at parties."

From a woman who always seems confident, the admission surprises me.

I cross to her bed and perch on the corner.

"Brooke. You're kind and funny and thoughtful and smart and the best friend a girl could ask for. I'm lucky to have you, and so's your brother."

One eye cracks open. "You mean it?"

I make a decision.

"Come on. Get dressed. We're going out."

"But aren't you meeting Clay after the game?" She sighs, batting her lashes up at me.

"This is more important."

Her expression brightens. "You want to hang out with me more than your baller boyfriend?"

"Yes, I do."

I wrap my arms around her shoulders, and a second later, she hugs me back. "Thanks," she murmurs into my shoulder.

I leave her in her walk-in closet with strict instructions not to come out until she's wearing something wild and head to my own room to find something.

When I'm flipping through outfits, I hit Clay's contact and cradle my phone against my shoulder.

"Couldn't wait?" his low, rumbling voice answers.

"Change of plans tonight. Brooke needs a friend."

"What happened?" Clay's concerned, and that makes me fall for him a little harder.

"It'll be fine, just girl stuff. We're going to hit a bar and dance and drink and complain about school friends."

"Tell me the name of the bar. I'll stop by."

My hand stills on the hanger of a dress. It would be fun to have him there, especially if he brought some of the guys. But that might not be the best given Brooke's current state of mind.

"I think she wants a simple night out. No Kodiaks."

When silence comes down the line, I'm worried he took it personally.

"There'll be a bottle of champagne waiting with her name on it. Plus a car to take you there and back," he says gruffly.

My lips tug up. "Just a simple night out, huh?" I tease.

"That's my compromise, Pink. You go out without me, I'm making sure you're looked after."

"Thank you." His gesture makes my chest ache. I tug the dress off the hanger, hold it up in front of me in the mirror. "You're not mad?"

"No. Text me when you get home."

My lips curve. "I will."

I tug my shirt over my head and kick off my leggings, glancing back at the mirror to see the cute lingerie I was planning on wearing for him.

"And in the meantime, I'll send you a picture to help you make it through."

"I'd appreciate that."

CLAY

"Finisher?" I uncork the bottle and take a sniff, grimacing. "How much are we getting paid to promote this?"

"It's part of the campaign to get you to the all-star game," my agent says.

I set the product on the conference table. "It's terrible."

"Bad enough you'd risk not getting to the all-star game?" Chloe demands.

I sling an arm over the back of the next chair. "I don't want to hawk shoe polish."

My agent says, "It's whisky, not shoe polish. You want anything sexier, it'll have to come in a paper bag."

I leave my meeting bottle in hand and swing by the wall where Nova's working. Since Christmas, we've been on the road and I've barely seen her.

Today she's not on the ladder but on her feet, working at the bottom of the wall.

I stop beside her and inspect her work. The mural is more than halfway done. The skyline is crisp and clear, and she's putting final touches on the starters.

My girl has a talent, that's for sure.

"Needs more muscle," I decide.

Nova looks up and beams. "You're back."

"I'm back."

Nova presses up on her toes and throws her arms around my neck—at least as far as they'll go given our height difference.

I inhale her scent. I missed the hell out of her. I miss her smile, her laugh, her brightness. I feel more whole just being in her presence.

Another couple employees are at the end of the hall, and I wait until they're barely gone to lift her and swing her around. When I set her back down, my fingers thread into her hair as I drag her mouth up to mine and kiss her thoroughly.

"What's that?" she asks breathlessly when I pull back and she notices the bottle.

"My ticket to the all-star game."

"Cute." She grins, clearly pleased. "Finisher? Most guys don't have a problem finishing."

"Uh-huh. I can last longer than you, Pink. Tonight, I'll prove it to you. Multiple times."

She bites her lip, reminding me it's been way too long since I had her alone. I'm a second away from dragging her to the nearest closet.

"What does it mean if you make the all-star team?" she asks.

It's an earnest question. Sometimes I feel so at ease around her that I forget how new she is to the sport.

"I go to all-star weekend. Play in the big game. See guys from all across the league. Talk shit. Party."

"So, it's like a high school sleepover for athletes."

A laugh rumbles through me. "Sure." I rub a hand over her head, and she ducks away.

Fuck, this girl is good for my soul. She keeps my ego in check, at least a little bit, and I love seeing the world through her eyes.

I want her to soften my edges while I rough up hers.

"Come with me," I ask on impulse. "It would mean a lot if you were there."

Her eyes widen. "But you haven't gotten in yet."

"Details. I've been an all-star the last three years I was healthy, Pink."

"Where is it?" she asks.

"LA."

Her smile fades a degree. "It's one thing to go to your games, but it'll raise questions if I show up there in your jersey. The all-star game isn't a Kodiaks thing—it's a Clayton Wade thing."

I set the bottle on the ladder and hook both thumbs in my pockets.

"I don't want to hide anymore. Not because it's anyone's business, but because it feels so good knowing you're mine, and I hate the thought of pretending that's not true."

Her lips part in surprise.

It's been a long time since I was with someone I felt serious about, and the last time, I got burned.

She's the best part of my day. I want everyone to know it.

I've been thinking about it every day I've been on planes and in other teams' stadiums.

As for Harlan, I'm going to tell him the truth.

He has to understand my relationship with Nova has nothing to do with basketball.

I want the career of my dreams and this woman in my bed and at my side.

Nova's phone buzzes before she can respond.

"It's Brooke. She's been stressed lately about these sorority girls. I better get it in case she needs something." She reaches for it and clicks Accept while I resist the urge to hurl the thing down the hall so she's forced to react to me first. "Hey, what's up?"

Brooke's garbled voice comes through the phone. Nova's eyes widen.

She lowers the phone and hits the speaker button. "My wall is on social media."

I look over her shoulder and watch the video of her work. Judging from how close it is to how the wall looks now, it was taken recently. "When'd you post that?"

"I didn't."

"Well, it has a hundred thousand views already." Brooke's voice comes through the speaker.

"Why would someone do that?" Nova asks.

"Free publicity," I supply.

"But this is the only post on their account. It's not following any others." Nova clicks a spot on the screen. "I've got DMs from all kinds of places."

"New fans. You don't have to read 'em all," I tell her. "I used to try to, but I wouldn't have time to practice, and then I'd have a hell of a lot less fans."

"Not just fans," Brooke counters. "You should read them, Nova."

Nova holds up the phone so I can read it as she says, "It's a gallery in New York inquiring about exhibiting some of my work. This is probably fake, right?" She lifts her face to mine, seeming genuinely perplexed.

I pull out my phone and do a quick search. "Name matches. Their account has a big following."

"They want to know if I can meet them. In person."

"Tell them yes," Brooke instructs. "If they'll cover your expenses, they're probably legit."

Nova types in the message window. Seconds later, someone is typing a response.

"They can send me a ticket to go this weekend," she says excitedly.

"If you need a travel buddy, I'm there," Brooke says before clicking off.

Nova looks up at me. "I've always wanted to see New York. Should I go?"

I've been looking forward to this weekend with her for the last two weeks.

But I'm not gonna crush this for her.

"Yeah," I say. "Of course you should. You'd love Central Park. No flowers this time of year, but it's still cool. And there's skating at Rockefeller Center."

She frowns, reading my hesitation. "Wait. When do you guys leave for your next road game?"

"Tuesday."

Her face falls. "Oh."

I tug her closer. "Go to New York with Brooke. Blow their minds."

17

NOVA

"*H*ow did it go?" Brooke demands as I answer my cell on my way out of the gallery.

"Good and bad." I exhale hard as I start along West 24th. "He asked about taking my pieces this summer, possibly for an entire exhibition."

"That's fantastic."

I've never had someone sit me down and talk seriously about my career and future before. The gallery was small but beautiful, and the pieces on display blew my mind.

"But he only deals in sports art. I think I'd like to branch out." I tug my collar closer to brace against the brisk wind.

"Brand is everything. You can attach yourself to this niche, Nova, then do whatever you want."

The possibility is thrilling.

Growing up, I thought I saw the world by moving from place to place in a trailer. Now, I realize I only saw part of it: the landscapes and small towns, not the style and the wealth I've seen since I first came to Denver for my sister's wedding.

It's not better, only different.

I check the map to see how I get to our meeting point.

"Are you heading to Neiman Marcus?" she asks.

"Yeah. I'll be there in five minutes."

When I get to Brooke, she embraces me.

"One of the girls from my sorority works here."

She introduces me, and the other woman reaches for my hand, displaying a huge diamond.

"Wow, you're engaged?" Brooke asks.

"Mhmm. You seeing anyone special?"

Brooke tosses her hair. "I have a bunch of guys I'm testing." She eyes up a few racks and mannequins and gestures to a bunch of items. "We want to try those."

"I'm afraid we only have one VIP dressing room."

"We'll share."

We're shown to a private dressing room as big as a bedroom.

"Think she'd wear that ring on her forehead if she could?" Brooke asks under her breath.

My lips curve. "She did seem proud of it. You could buy yourself one if you wanted."

"I don't want to settle down. Being tethered to a guy forever is my nightmare. But it drives me crazy how some of the girls from school lord it over other people." She shudders. "What about you? You and Clay seem to be getting cozy. As much as I'm not the biggest cheerleader for relationships, I've never seen him make so much effort."

My heart skips, and I glance back at my friend. "Really?"

"Oh yeah. It's the way he looks at you. The way he looks for you when you're not next to him."

I shimmy into a dress and check out my reflection. "He wants to tell the world about us."

"And you don't want to?"

I turn the idea over. "I thought I did. But maybe I've gotten used to the privacy? I like that our relationship is ours and no one else's business. The other day, I finished painting early and stopped by to see him after the game. There was a

196

line of people wanting selfies and autographs, wanting to just be around him. If we come out to the world, it's a big deal. Not only for friends and family, but it's an actual story just because it's Clay."

"When you're in public, people are in your business, but that doesn't mean they know your business. They don't know what goes on between you, and they don't have to."

I think about making him laugh and smile.

I love how hard he works, how kind he is to those who need help, especially when no one's looking.

I've started imagining a future with him, not just nights and days but birthdays and anniversaries.

"What are you afraid of?" Brooke asks.

My gaze meets hers. "I'm falling for him."

Her grin is slow and wide. "Obviously."

Shock slams into me. "It's obvious to you or to him?"

"To me because I'm smarter than your boy toy."

I reach for the zipper and work it down. "So, if you're not a romantic, why are you rooting for this?"

"Because you're my friend and I want everyone to love you as much as I do. Plus, these guys are used to having control of everything and it's fun to watch them spiral."

I toss a shirt at her, and she catches it, laughing.

The more I think about it, the more I like it.

I'll tell Clay I'm good with announcing us, that he doesn't have to worry about pressuring me. I trust him.

"I'm not sure we'll have time after we get back tomorrow. He's heading away on another road trip."

Brooke grins. "Then let's go back early."

"Have you seen Clay?" I ask Rookie outside the Kodiaks locker room.

He waves down the hallway toward the court.

Brooke and I got back in record time. Since our talk, all I can think about is seeing Clay.

My chest has been stretched so tight it feels as if my heart is going to beat out from within my ribs.

After landing, I showered and headed to the stadium, figuring I'd find Clay there.

I follow the winding hallway toward the court, replaying what I'd rehearsed in my mind.

When I get to the end of the tunnel, I hear Clay's voice, hushed but urgent.

"...need to talk about our deal."

"The deal where I agreed I'd get you to LA?" Harlan's voice cuts in, every bit as tight but with an edge of frustration.

I pull up out of sight. This must be related to what they were fighting about at Christmas.

"You didn't hold up your end of the bargain," Harlan says.

"It wasn't my fault she came back."

The hairs on my neck lift.

"No, but you were supposed to stay away from her when she did."

My heart stops.

I can't believe what I'm hearing.

I want to run, but I can't bring myself to do it.

Instead, I step into the hallway.

They both turn to face me. Clay's expression is tight with shock, Harlan's surprised and guilty.

"Who were you supposed to stay away from?" I ask as steadily as I can.

"Nova. I thought you were in New York," Clay says, but Harlan clears his throat.

"You. He was supposed to stay away from you."

No.

"Why?" My voice trembles at the edges.

"Because it would be easier for everyone." Harlan again.

I turn toward him, my hands clenching into fists at my sides. "You're supposed to be family. I trusted you, and you manipulated me."

His jaw tightens. "Nova, that's not what—"

"Mari always did growing up, but at least she was my sister. Who are you to manage my life?"

He doesn't answer.

"And you." I round to face Clay, intending to confront him with all my anger.

But looking at him has emotions rushing up at me in a wave.

The backs of my eyes burn, and I spin and bolt out of the building.

Clay's on my heels. "Nova. Nova, wait."

He catches up to me outside the front doors, his trainers getting wet in the snow. I look up at him, not hiding the tears burning my eyes.

"It's not what you think."

"How do you know what I think?" I take a shaky breath.

"Let me explain."

"That you made some kind of a bargain with Harlan that involved my feelings and your career?"

His throat works, his expression a tight mask of misery and hurt. "I told you I panicked that night, about us. That was true."

"So, you went over my head and decided we were done without consulting me."

"When you put it like that, it sounds bad."

My eyes widen. "It took me putting it like that to make it sound bad?!"

Clay rubs his hands over his face. "I'm sorry."

The next breath is painful. I wanted to tell him I was ready to go public, and now everything we had feels like it was built on a lie. I finally felt as if we were on even ground but he was treating me like a child this entire time.

"Me too."

I shut my eyes briefly, as if that can block out the emotions raging through me, but when I open them, all the hurt and disappointment and anger are right there bubbling at the surface.

"You think you know better than everyone. On the court and off it. But you don't get to decide what's best, Clay."

He reaches for me as though it's the most natural thing in the world, as though it's his right to touch me and he can fix everything if we're closer.

Part of me wants that too, which is why I force myself to step back.

His hands fall back to his sides, his dark eyes bright with anguish as he wrestles with his control.

"I didn't expect to see you before I left on this road trip. I don't want to waste it. Let me take you out tonight. We can talk about this."

Yes.

I hate having barriers between me and the people I care about.

That's how all of this started, wanting to be on good terms with my sister.

But...

That's my old pattern. I don't want to cave, to be the one who bends simply because I'm better at it. I want to stand up for myself.

"It sounds like you've been doing enough talking for both of us," I say and start toward the street.

This time, he doesn't come after me.

18

NOVA

"*N*ova."

I turn to see James Parker standing behind me in a sport coat and jeans, his lean face tight.

I pull off my headphones. "Hi."

The past few days, I've thrown myself into working on the mural.

The guys on the court are coming together. It's less of a literal rendition, the style implying energy and speed and connection.

I haven't seen Clay since I caught him and Harlan in the hallway. He's texted me multiple times, but I don't feel I'm ready to talk.

Focusing on my art is hard when it involves the

man I've fallen for and am not speaking to, but I try to forget that part.

"I'm still working on the third element," I tell James. "If there's a problem with the mural…"

"The problem isn't how the wall looks—it's that there's a leak. You leaked it."

My brows shoot up as I remember the photo from over a week ago. "I didn't."

"We have a big reveal at the gala. Our contract stated that this remained confidential."

"And I've abided by that," I assure him. "It could have been anyone. All the players and staff have access to the wall."

"All of whom have been instructed not to share it and none of whom have motive to do so. I've been more than generous renegotiating the terms of our arrangement."

I'm sure Clay would say fair, but whatever.

"I understand this gala means a lot to you."

"It's more than a lot. The Kodiaks were an expansion team no one thought would survive in the league. Since I bought them, I've turned them into a contender."

"I'm sure everyone in the organization wants to make it a success."

He frowns. "It's my name on the door."

"Are you the one scoring the points too?" I joke.

He doesn't smile.

"Everyone in this building serves at my discretion. When they no longer suit me, they will be removed. I don't want us to be in that position. Do you understand?"

His words have the effect of a bucket of ice water over my head.

I square my shoulders and look him in the eye.

"Yes. Yes, I think I do."

I'm starting to get the feeling this gala isn't even about the team—it's about him.

Mari looks up from the stove where she's cooking. "Pass me the parmesan."

I hand her the grated cheese, and she tosses a bunch in, then some more.

"I thought dairy caused problems?" I ask, surprised.

"Honestly, I've been craving it lately."

"James was such a prick," I say, waving my half-full glass of wine.

"Harlan doesn't much like him either," she admits.

"I figured. But I expected you to say something like, 'Money makes the world go 'round, Nova.'"

She cocks her head, reaching for her own wine. "I don't sound like that."

"You do a little."

Her eyes roll, and I find a smile.

"James is bored and trying to make his mark somewhere. His family made headlines for their business acumen, and he wants to see his name in the papers too."

"I didn't leak the photos. You don't think James did it himself?"

"No. The fact that these got out without him knowing pissed him off, but probably more was the fact his name wasn't mentioned once."

"Then someone else must've done it, probably as a prank."

When Mari asked me over for dinner, I jumped at it.

"I do have good news," I say. "This gallery owner in New York wants to have an exhibition of my art."

"Really?!"

"Mhmm. I wasn't sure if I was going to take it,

but with the way James is talking, I need to start figuring out my next steps."

"You never liked an ultimatum. When we were six or seven, you were running around naked, and Mom and Dad told you to put your clothes on for dinner or you could swim in the lake the entire time we were gone and we'd pick you up after. You dove back in without a second glance."

"It backfired. Even though there was a lifeguard, Mom went to get hot dogs, and all of you had to stay at the beach and eat on a blanket."

"It was fun," she says, grinning. "What made you stop being that girl?"

"A lot of things." I take a big gulp of wine. "Mom and Dad dying. You always making the right moves. I started to feel like I wasn't helping things by going my own direction. So, I tried to go with the flow instead of making waves."

She grabs my arm. "You can make waves with me."

I smile.

Mari looks at my almost-empty glass. "We need a new bottle," she insists, though she's barely touched hers. "Want to go grab one?"

"What kind?"

"Whatever you like."

I bounce down to the cellar and select two reds at random.

"Mar, I brought a spare in case one is from a fifteenth-century monastery and being saved for you and Harlan's first-born or something…"

I trail off as I see her standing over the island, staring at the marble surface, the wooden spoon dripping onto the floor.

She holds up my phone. "Nova. Who is this?"

Grumpy Baller: I miss the fuck out of you. Can't sleep without you here.

My stomach drops.

"Please tell me it's not one of Harlan's players. Miles likes to flirt, but you know better than—"

"It's not Miles. It's Clay."

Her mouth falls open. "Nova. He's an asshole."

I set both wine bottles on the island and take a breath. "He's a good guy. You don't know him, not really. All anyone knows is what he presents to the media in interviews."

"You don't have the best track record for judgment."

"You liked Brad too." I turn one of the bottles before setting it down again.

"So, you're sleeping with him."

I square my shoulders. "I'm in love with him."

She inhales sharply. "Nova... don't say that."

"You think I don't know my own heart?" There's an edge to my voice.

"I think when it comes to your heart or your head, your heart wins every time."

"You fell for Harlan and got married six months later," I counter.

"But I know him inside and out. It was a thought-out decision."

Another text comes in.

Grumpy Baller: Harlan and I had a talk. He promised to keep it quiet as long as you need.

Mari's eyes narrow. "Harlan knows?"

Dammit.

Her expression goes pale with shock or rage— I'm not sure which.

"We don't keep secrets, Nova. We didn't before you."

It feels like she's slapped me.

"I know you're upset, Mar, but this isn't my fault."

I wanted to bond with my sister, and now I've made things more difficult by being here.

When I think it can't get any worse, the door to the garage sounds.

"Hello?"

Harlan.

Mari stomps past me to her husband in the foyer. His suit hangs impeccably, but he looks tired —until he sees her and his eyes crinkle.

"It's good to see you."

"How long did you know about Clay and Nova?"

He looks between us, his expression tightening.

"Maybe I should go," I murmur.

Harlan speaks first. "Maybe you should."

19

CLAY

The week passes in a blur of airplanes and workouts and other teams' stadiums. Two road games later, we're back on the plane heading to Denver.

We lost both games.

On the plane, the pitch-black sky invites the worst kind of thoughts.

Miles watches a video on his phone, sneaking looks at me.

"What?" I grunt, grabbing the phone from his hand.

It's a clip of me picking a fight with Coach after the third quarter, when he got in my face about my performance. Not because my stat line was in a nosedive, though it was, but because I wasn't helping my team run the schemes to keep us in it.

Microphones on the video pick up his comments.

"I don't care if you can't get a bucket. Get downhill, pass it out, and get these guys running."

And mine.

"I'm paid too much to pass all night."

"You're paid too much *not* to."

Instead of falling into line, I got toe to toe with Coach and ripped him a new one.

I was frustrated over Nova and lost my head, letting it all out on someone I shouldn't have.

He benched me in the fourth.

Didn't stop me from getting in his face after the microphones were gone.

"Easy for you to tell us what we should be doing, to act like you've got all the answers," I ground out. "Said yourself you're no better than a pawn between James and Harlan. Either one of them could snap their fingers and fire you. Yeah, you're real brave."

I expected him to fine me on the spot.

Instead, he got quiet and walked out. After the game, in the visitors' locker room, I informed Chloe I wasn't going to do media.

"You weren't invited," she replied briskly.

Nova and I haven't spoken in days, and it's been fucking terrible.

Half a dozen texts to check in on her, none answered.

I don't hate that she found out, but it's how she found out. I was planning to tell her about my deal with Harlan.

But only after I worked out a way to tell Harlan —and everyone—about us.

My head falls back against the leather seat. Emotions claw at my chest, raking talons that reach beneath my ribs to the places I can't protect with ego or reputation or silence.

She's hurting, and I can't fix it.

Not if she won't answer my texts.

Not when I'm on a plane a thousand miles away.

I need her to understand I wasn't trying to manipulate her.

A year ago, all I wanted was for my knee to hold up.

It's been solid for weeks.

So, why does it feel like my life is crumbling?

"I fucked up," I say.

Miles shifts forward, glancing around the

plane. The rest of the team is locked in one-on-one conversations, or sleeping, or watching videos, or listening to music.

"The guys will give you another chance," he says.

"It's not the guys I'm worried about," I admit.

We're practicing the next day, running plays with the assistant, when Miles calls out, "Where's Coach?"

I glance at the clock in the corner of the gym. It's not like him to be late.

I head to the bleachers and grab my phone from my bag. No messages. I punch in his contact.

It rings.

Again.

Voicemail picks up.

"Get your ass here, old man, I'm doing your job and mine. You're gonna want to take a picture because it's not happening again." I click off and rejoin practice.

It's not an apology, but it's halfway there.

I crossed a line with Coach. Took shit out on him that wasn't his fault.

I'll make it up to him today.

Jayden and the assistant coaches run the team through some drills while I watch.

A few minutes later, Rookie pulls up, looking past me.

"Clay."

The voice at my back is familiar, but the name isn't. Harlan never calls me Clay.

I straighten, immediately alert. *Something's wrong.*

"What happened?"

The hospital is a mass of hallways and hurrying staff and beeping equipment. My steps overtake the nurse leading us in.

Jay and Miles and Atlas look at me with hollow eyes. Behind them is a row of assistant coaches.

I hate hospitals. My little sister spent too much time in one, and I couldn't do anything for her. I threw myself into my game because living with the idea that I had no impact was insufferable.

We all wait for an hour.

Two.

Harlan arrives looking tired already. "Thank

you all for coming. We don't have the full details, but we understand Coach's car went off the road and hit a tree late this afternoon. The doctors believe it may have resulted from a cardiac incident, but as a result, he's sustained significant trauma to multiple systems. I understand how much Coach means to you. He'd appreciate knowing you were here."

"He'll know once he's out," Jay insists.

"That won't be for some time. In the interim, you should go home and rest," Harlan says.

One at a time, the guys peel off. Miles first, then Atlas. Rookie. Jayden. The coaching staff too.

I keep pacing the room. Still in my hoodie over a practice jersey, plus shorts, my Kobes on my feet.

"You won't get to see him tonight."

I look up to meet Harlan's eyes.

He rests a hand on my shoulder, but I shrug it off. My attention goes to my knee, the scar there.

Harlan retreats and returns a moment later with faded blue polyester folded in his hands. "At least put these on so you don't freeze."

Harlan leaves me with the scrubs. I drop them on the chair and do laps of the ward. People spot me, but the nurses don't care.

I'm not famous here. I have no power.

I return to the nurse's station. "Let me see him."

"You can't right now, Mr. Wade." She frowns.

I rub a hand over my face. "I need to see him."

She starts to argue, but another nurse clears her throat. "You can go in."

I head into the room full of beeping machines. He's lying in the bed, tubes and monitors hooked up everywhere. For once, he's quiet.

There's no chair, so I get one from the hallway and carry it in.

NOVA

The past week, I've been going to the wall.

Literally.

The mural has consumed my waking moments.

But when Brooke came home looking stricken and told me about Coach, I couldn't sit at home.

Twenty minutes later, I'm at the hospital. Through some emotional appeal, the nurses finally allow me in.

Clay is slouched in a tiny visitor's chair at his coach's bedside.

In the bed, the man who always looked sprightly and energetic is still and pale.

The anger and betrayal I felt seem small compared to the scene in front of me.

I rest a hand on Clay's shoulder. "Hi."

He doesn't respond.

I start to pull back, but Clay's hand covers mine. "Hi."

"How is he?" I ask.

"Not good." The words are barely audible.

"How long have you been here?"

"Since practice. Harlan tried to get me to leave." When his hand falls away, I miss it.

"Harlan was right." It's after midnight.

"It was my fault," he goes on as if he didn't hear me.

My arms wrap around my body. I'm only now realizing I didn't put on a coat before coming over.

"You weren't driving."

"No, but I gave him hell the other day."

"Your words didn't give him a heart attack, or steer him off the road. No one's that powerful. Not even Clayton Wade."

He tilts his head up to look at me.

I'm still upset with him, but the downward

spiral is familiar. Clay seems intent to stay here all night, which won't help anyone.

I make an executive decision. "We're leaving. Give me your keys."

I hold out a hand, and after a long moment, Clay reaches into his pocket and passes over the fob.

I lead the way out of the hospital. Normally heading through a busy building would mean people snapping pics of Clay, but today, everyone we pass is either sick or working.

Fame can't trump illness.

We reach the parking lot, and Clay nods toward the section holding his SUV.

"I can drive," he says.

"I don't care what you think you can do," I bite out.

His eyes widen in surprise, but when I round to the driver's seat and get in, he shifts into the other side.

After sliding into his SUV, I move the seat forward a foot and adjust the mirrors.

"I'm sorry." His voice fills the dark.

"Apologize to Coach when he wakes up."

"I mean about the deal with Harlan. I'm sorry I

made you think I didn't trust you to choose for yourself."

The words settle on me, seeping into my skin. I don't have time to guard against them, and there's no protection from the raw emotion in his voice.

"Tonight's not about us."

I drive him home.

The roads are dark and quiet. I don't put on the radio.

When we pull up to the building, the garage door lifts automatically. From memory, I navigate to the spot right next to the elevator.

We ride up together, and I sneak a look at him in the fluorescent lights.

I've never seen him like this.

He's always strong.

Now, he's suffering.

I know what it's like to have someone ripped from your life with zero notice. To be talking to them one moment, laughing or arguing or debating, and the next they're gone.

That's why I won't let him face this alone, no matter what's between us.

The wide hallway is lined with subtle, expensive lights. Clay takes his keys back and unlocks the door. The lights click on automatically to reveal the familiar, beautifully decorated space. The foyer leads into the white granite-swathed kitchen and, on the other side, the massive living room with low couches and a huge TV.

"Are you hungry? Thirsty?"

He shakes his head.

I take in what he's wearing. His knee looks swollen. "You should ice that."

"Later."

"At least have a shower."

Clay pulls his sweatshirt off over his head, the jersey beneath coming with it.

An angry purple splotch has my breath catching. "What happened?"

"I dunno."

I stroke a finger across it. He seems strong, but he's human too.

I walk through his place to the master bedroom and bathroom. The light turns on when I step inside. I reach the shower and turn the handle.

Behind me, he stands stock still, his gaze fixed partway down the wall. I start to brush past him, but he grabs my wrist.

"Don't go." His thumb strokes my pulse point. His gorgeous dark eyes are full of fear and guilt and regret. "I know I don't deserve it. But I can't watch you leave. Not tonight."

He wraps me in his arms, crushing me hard to his chest. My heart hammers between us, my eyes stinging with tears.

In the time we've been together, he's never hugged me. If you can even call this a hug. It's like he's clinging to a rock to avoid being swept out to sea.

I know what it's like to lose people and blame yourself. I want to hold him here for as long as I can.

"I care about you. So fucking much," he rumbles into my neck. "You wanted your sister back and a fresh start. I'm a lightning rod and a mess. Your best shot was staying far away from me."

His words gut me. I know he believes he was helping, even if that was a fucked-up way to do it.

The tattoos twining around his arms and chest could be ropes tying him down.

I'm not ready to let it go, but I can't retreat from him either. It's harder and harder to keep up my guard, even if my heart will get bruised.

"I didn't want to stay away from you," I

whisper against his bare chest. My fingers dig into the smooth skin of his back.

Clay swallows hard enough that I feel it.

"Me either."

It's not your fault, I want to tell him.

I show him instead.

20

CLAY

I wake to the sun coming in the gap at the bottom of my curtains.

In a dark wave, it all comes rushing back.

Coach's accident.

Pacing the hospital for hours.

Him hooked up to machines, silent and lifeless.

Cutting through the darkness, Nova driving me home.

She's next to me, her skin warm and soft.

She's my strength.

When I was drowning, it was her face that appeared over me.

She let me hold her for fucking hours, slept next to me while I tossed and turned.

I love her.

Thoroughly and fucking completely.

The realization isn't a lightning bolt but a steady truth, one that's been humming in my veins for longer than I knew.

My phone buzzes on the bedside table. I exhale when I see the caller ID. I shift out of bed and pull on gray sweatpants, taking the phone to the other room so I don't wake Nova.

"Yeah," I answer as I pull the door shut after me.

Harlan's voice comes down the line. "Wade. I've talked with James, and we want you to address the team."

"Why not Jayden?"

"We want Coach to have privacy at this time. Chloe's issuing a statement to say that he's out for personal reasons," he goes on as though I didn't ask. "But first, you need to talk to them."

"And say what? They were there."

"That our lead assistant coach will be taking over as head coach. Indefinitely."

I stiffen. "Why not acting?" He doesn't answer. "Whose fucking idea was this? Yours or James'?"

"It was mutual."

"Bullshit." I hear the truth in his voice. Parker gets off on moving pieces around, looking like a big boy. This is him doing that. "Coach will be back. It could be today."

"I need you to put the team first right now."

Nova comes out of the bedroom, my T-shirt clinging to her curves and ending at her knees.

She cocks her head.

"Harlan," I mouth.

Her lips press together.

Yeah, this situation isn't resolved, but I need to resolve it.

She heads for the washroom, the door clicking behind her.

"Is that Nova?" Harlan asks. A lucky guess.

"Yeah, it is." My grip tightens on the phone. "Make no mistake, I want her in my life, and I'm gonna do whatever it takes to make that happen. If you've got a problem with her or me or us, you can tell me right the fuck now. Because this is a fight you're going to lose."

Harlan exhales. "Not today."

I cross my living room and hit the blinds. The morning sun is exposed an inch at a time.

"We need to talk about LA," he says.

The light at the end of the tunnel.

The reason for every decision I made this past year.

"Not today." I echo his words before clicking off.

Nova emerges, her face bright as if she just washed it and her hair pulled up into a pink knot on her head. Blue eyes search mine as she crosses the carpet to me.

"Any news?" she asks.

I cross to her and wrap an arm around her waist to tug her against me. "Just that the assistant coach is taking over."

"That makes sense." She tips her face back to hold my eyes.

"Only if Coach isn't coming back from this. Parker couldn't wait an entire news cycle." The tightness in my chest is back.

But Nova shakes her head. "Harlan thinks this team is more than any one person. Coach knows that too. Everyone's trying to do the best they can."

I frown, leaning my forehead against hers. "You always think about other people."

"It's not that hard," she murmurs, her lips curving.

"Sometimes it is. When you've lived your life thinking it's you against the world, it is."

Her eyes soften as she looks up at me.

"I heard what you said to Harlan about us," she says.

My breath catches. "And?"

"I liked it."

The knot in my chest loosens a bit. "I meant it. I know I'm really fucking good at basketball, but when it comes to being a good boyfriend...I guess I'm starting from zero."

"Possibly less than zero, after what you and Harlan did," she points out, but her lips twitch.

"The fact you're still here mean you've forgiven me?" I suggest.

She pulls back an inch, suspicious. "I didn't say that."

I lift her off her feet and toss her over my shoulder.

She screeches, grabbing my shoulders for balance. "I need to go to work!"

"Guess what, Nova? It's Saturday, and it's been a rough week. My girl just told me I need to do better. So I'm going to practice."

"Wait!"

"Wasn't a request."

I lock my arm around the backs of her thighs and stalk toward my bedroom. She squirms but gives up the moment I drag up the shirt and bury my face between those thighs.

For hours, I forget all the bad shit.

21

CLAY

For the past week, Coach has been in a coma and I've been doing what Harlan asked.

I talk to the team.

I put on a good act.

I'm at the gym even earlier than usual, keeping an eagle eye on practice for when the assistant coaches screw up.

Today, while I'm trying to keep spirits up at practice, I see someone I don't expect hovering at the edge of the tunnel.

James Parker stands straight as rod, hands in his pockets as we run drills.

The second I get rotated out, I grab a Gatorade and head for him.

"Clay. What a pleasure."

From his voice, it's clear my presence is anything but.

"You could've waited more than a day before giving away Coach's job," I say as I stop in front of him.

"A team needs a head coach. A conscious one too. The league is demanding like that," he drawls. "My hands are tied."

"Your hands are meddling."

"You're six-five, but you think you have better perspective than I do up there?" He nods to his office in the rafters of the building.

I pop the top on my drink. "I think you're so far away you can't tell a basketball from a breadbasket." I chug half the bottle, enjoying the way his face contorts. "If you want to win a championship in this town, stay out of shit you don't understand. That includes Nova."

"Nova?" He cocks his head, genuinely surprised.

She told me about his threats.

"She didn't leak any pictures of the wall, so stop trying to take advantage of her."

He smiles, genuine delight edging into his expression. "When we brought you here, you were a killer. You're losing your edge."

"Fuck with me and we'll find out."

An outburst from the court makes me look up.

"Shit!"

"Fucking yes!"

The guys are gathered around a phone.

I jog over to them.

"Practice over?" I drawl.

"Clay! You made the all-star team," Jay says.

I straighten, palming the ball in one hand. This past week, I'd all but forgotten about the timeline to name participants in the game.

The guys swarm me, throwing their arms around me and hitting me with their towels.

"I made it." Pride rushes up through my chest.

When I look over, James is gone from the tunnel. I push him from my mind as Jay comes up beside me.

"Gentlemen, Mr. Clayton Wade has been selected for the all-star team! Let's give him a round of applause!"

Amidst the whistles and cheers from the other players, I just stand there, relishing the moment. This is what I've worked so hard for—to be recognized as one of the best basketball players in the league.

For a moment, my worries about the future melt away.

"It's a big deal!" Nova exclaims over the phone. Her enthusiasm lights me up.

"I've been a bunch of times," I say into my car's hands-free speaker.

"Doesn't matter, Clay. You're one in a million."

"Twenty-four of three hundred," I say because, what the hell? I've never been humble, might as well try it on for size.

"You'll have to come home and celebrate."

Home. The word hits me hard.

I never thought of my condo as home since I bought it a year ago, but hearing her say the word makes it sound appealing.

My home. Hers. Ours.

We're in a strange in-between spot. With Coach in the hospital, we lean on one another, but we're still rebuilding the trust between us.

Yesterday, when she came over, we watched a movie and she spent the night curled in my arms.

I want to tell her how I feel about her, but it's a

weird time to do it. Coach's hospitalization hangs over all of us, and the mood is tense.

"Listen, I should stop in to see Coach on the way," I say as I turn off the road and into a drive-through. "You don't have to wait up."

"I want to."

Damn if I'm not grateful for that.

When I click off with Nova, I pull up to the ordering window.

"Lettuce, no tomato. Double pickles. Triple hot sauce."

"Triple?" the woman asks, sounding startled.

"Yeah."

I take the paper bags to the hospital, navigating through the halls with my hands full.

I enter Coach's room, settle into the chair that barely holds me, and pull out the dinners.

"Jay's thumb is bugging him on his threes, but he won't admit it. I'm trying to take away some of his reps without him noticing, which is hard as fuck. Atlas's free throws are up ten percent. He draws more fouls, we might get somewhere this year."

I bite into my burger, chewing and swallowing before I go through my mental notes on every other player on the Kodiaks.

Who knows if Coach can hear me, but I wouldn't put it past him.

And when he wakes up, he's going to be pissed if he's out of the loop.

The phone rings, the shrill sound too loud in this place. I grab it. *Harlan.*

"I understand you're going to the all-star game."

"I understand you might be divorced by next week."

Nova told me about her sister finding out—that we were together, and that Harlan kept it from her.

He sighs. "Mari's upset. She'll get over it."

"That what happens when you fight?"

"I'm not sure. We don't usually fight."

Coach's breathing is even. His eyelids are paper-thin. He's always been hard and tough, but now he looks fragile.

Fragile things don't last in this world.

"LA put together a solid offer. They called me with it this morning." Harlan's words cut into my thoughts.

"I wasn't sure you'd still be pursuing that given everything going on."

"My responsibility is to this team, and your

stock is rising. The more you're worth, the more we can get back for you."

I expect to feel anticipation. Instead, the emotions swirling are complicated.

LA is still the top team in the West. But Nova's here. Coach is here. The guys I've gotten closer to this year, whether I meant to or not... I'd be leaving them.

"This is what you wanted," he reminds me. "Their GM's going to have it over to me in writing in a couple of days."

I clear my throat. "Let's talk about it after this weekend."

He's quiet for a minute. "We'll talk after."

I shift back in my chair and hang up.

Coach's hearing was always eerily accurate. He could decipher a muttered comment from across the gym.

"This what you want?" I ask him. "Team of my dreams is calling, and I'm busy bringing you takeout."

Coach is silent, the only sound the machines beeping softly.

"I mean it. You're not here to stop me, I might do something I regret." I nudge his calf with my toe and nod at his dinner, still wrapped. "Not usually a two burger guy, but that could change today."

In college during Final Four, Coach was coaching another team, and he saw I was fucked up. He told me to get in his car, and I did. We stopped for fast food, and I told him about my broken heart.

We kept in touch. He checked in on me over the years.

Let me lean on him more than once.

I cut him down because I was self-centered and impatient.

You can lean on me, I want to say. *Just wake the fuck up.*

I think about the time back in preseason when we were supposed to sing the team song and I refused.

I look around, seeing the lights click off on the floor as the staff prepare for the overnight shift. At the station across the hall, one of the nurses is humming under her breath.

"You want me to do it? Fine. I'll do it. But you tell Jay about this, I'll end you."

I lower my voice and sing.

22

NOVA

"*T*his is either the best idea ever or the worst," I whisper as Brooke and I creep down the hallway of the hotel. The cardboard cutout is clutched between us, the head under her armpit while I grab the feet.

"It's a tradition," Brooke replies.

"How can it be a tradition? I thought this was Miles' first time?"

I've learned there are a few ways to get an invitation to all-star weekend: as a player for the main game, as part of the skills night—like the dunk competition—or as part of the rookie game.

Earlier tonight were the skills competitions. The dunks were pretty spectacular, but we were there to cheer for the three-point competitors.

Especially Miles, who lit up the scoreboard to win with a near-perfect score.

We're almost to 1475, the room number Brooke told me in the stairwell as we prepped for this.

"What are you ladies doing with Michael?"

I look up, full of guilt, to see Jayden standing sternly over us.

"What do you think?" Brooke replies.

Jay pulls out his phone. "We gotta hurry. He's on his way back." He looks up and down the hall. "Let's go."

They exchange a grin that looks eerily similar. Brooke produces a key card she swipes at the door.

"I'm not asking how you got that," Jay muses.

"Better not."

"I thought all-star weekend was about, I dunno, basketball," I say.

They both laugh.

"It's an excuse to hang out with my boys across the league."

"What about for you?" I ask Brooke.

"I get to party and decide which of a few hundred attractive male specimens gets the prize of hooking up with me."

"You're not gonna hook up with someone," her brother objects. "Not now, not ever."

"I already have."

Jay straightens. "Tell me his name and I'll end him."

"Which year?" Brooke breezes into the room, leaving her brother muttering behind her.

I came to the all-star game to support Clay. Even if he's been before, it's a big deal. He asked me to stay with him, but I said no, wanting a little bit of space and also for him to have time with his guys.

Brooke and I are sharing a room, one I insisted on paying for with my latest paycheck from the Kodiaks.

But I am wearing the jersey Clay had delivered to my door—a special all-star edition bearing his name and number. It arrived with a handwritten note.

This one has a fireproof coating.

CW

"The bathroom?" I ask as Brooke and Jay head inside.

"Yeah. It has to be in the shower so when he

pulls the curtain back, there's Michael," Brooke explains.

They take turns positioning the cardboard cutout.

"No, wait, like this." Jay steps inside the shower with both feet, making the cutout assume an awkward and provocative position.

"Why Michael Bublé?" I ask.

"One year, Jay kept listening to what he called his hype music but wouldn't let anyone in on it. Turned out it was Michael Bublé's Christmas album. The guys never let him live it down," Brooke says under her breath.

We watch Jay step out of the bathtub and brush off his hands.

The sound of laugher in the hallway makes us freeze.

"Shit!" I curse.

There's no time to get out. Brooke grabs me and Jay and sprints out of the bathroom as voices stop outside the door.

There's nowhere to hide.

Jay dives into the closet, pulling it shut behind him.

"Traitor!" Brooke hisses.

Pulling her with me, I lunge for the curtains like people do in the movies.

The door clicks. I listen to him walk into the bathroom and turn on the sink.

"What the...?"

Brooke and I hold our breath in anticipation.

"This soap is fucking terrible."

We look at each other and laugh silently.

I peek out as Jay slips out of the closet and through the front door. Just when we start to creep toward the door, the faucet cuts out.

We run back to the curtains.

We're safe until we hear a little yip.

Waffles. I forgot all about Waffles.

He's sniffing Brooke's high heels with excitement.

"What is it, boy?"

The curtain jerks away, and Miles is standing there in a towel. "Well, what have we here?"

He's definitely cut, but Brooke's appreciating him enough for both of us.

"If you wanted to touch my trophy, all you had to do was ask," he says.

I swallow a laugh and duck toward the door, leaving them alone.

Outside, my gaze lands on Clay's door across the hall.

It opens and he peers out, doing a double take.

His arched brow when he sees me makes me want to bite my lip.

He's wearing sweatpants slung low on his hips, his shirt in one hand like he was in the middle of pulling it on.

Or taking it off.

God he's gorgeous. I should be over it after all this time, desensitized from being in the presence of that much hotness on a regular basis, but I'm not.

"Should I be jealous?" he murmurs, taking in where I've come from.

"Maybe," I tease.

"Of Miles or Michael?" he asks.

I throw up my hands. "Does everyone know about this?"

"They did it to me my first year. We weren't even on the same team."

His slow grin is contagious, and I can't stop the laughter that rises up.

My shoulders rock until tears warm the corners of my eyes.

A player I don't know heads down the hall, and he and Clay exchange a nod. I step closer to Clay to avoid being in the way and get a hint of his clean male scent.

"What are you doing in the players' hotel, pretty girl?" Clay murmurs near my ear.

My gaze runs over his muscles and tattoos, my throat going dry.

I peer up at him through my lashes and shrug out of my jacket to show him the jersey.

His jersey.

"I was hoping to get this signed."

His eyes darken. "Watch it. I'll write my name on you with permanent ink."

I bite my lip. "You already did that."

"That was my number. And I said I owed you a tattoo."

"You still do."

He goes back into his room and returns with a pen. "Where do you want it?"

I debate a second before I pull down the neck of my jersey, exposing my ribs over my heart.

Clay writes carefully across my skin. I'm not watching the pen—I'm watching him.

"Before you look at it, I need to tell you something." He clears his throat. "Everything I am, everything I did, was about basketball. The one time I faltered, the one time I blinked back in college, it burned me. Bad enough I swore I'd never hesitate again.

"Coach's accident got me thinking about how everyone in this hotel, in that arena, knows me for basketball. If I died tonight, that's what they'd remember me for. But I want more than that, Nova."

My breath catches.

"I want your brightness to rub off on me... and maybe some of your goodness too. It's not fair to ask that of you, but what I can promise you in return is that I'll care about you. I'll put you first. I'm not used to that, so I'm going to screw it up, but I want to do it."

I look down at my chest, at the words he wrote carefully on my skin.

I love you

CW

It doesn't feel like fireworks. More like balloons lifting off from the ground, drawing me weightlessly up with them.

There's never been a time I wasn't drawn to Clay, from the very first moment when we argued over a seat on a plane I didn't want to take.

He believed in me when no one else did. His quiet confidence taught me how to believe in myself.

My heart has cracked open, sprouted new buds and blossoms thanks to him.

"Okay," I say.

"Okay? What the hell does that mean," he growls.

"It means I love you too."

His eyes work back and forth over mine, his jaw clenching.

Clay's hands fist at his sides. "You're serious."

The silence between us is buzzing. Or maybe it's the blood pounding in my ears as we stare at each other.

I smile so wide it hurts. "Way serious. Now can I please come in?"

He grabs the back of my neck and hauls me towards him.

23

CLAY

"*W*on't everyone know?" Nova says as I tug her inside.

"You got Michael into Miles's room. I can get you into mine."

She laughs as she surveys my room, lifting the lid of the silver pail on the fridge. "Huh. There's even ice in the bucket."

There could be a groundhog living in the thing and I wouldn't blink.

Nova loves me.

The woman I've been falling for since the moment she crashed into my life just said she feels the same.

After holding everyone at a distance for my entire life, now, my chest might explode.

Nova opens the drapes and peers outside. "Remember the last time we did this?"

"I told Rookie if he came to my balcony tonight, I'd push him off." I come up behind her, and her body warms me. I place my hands on either side of her, my groin pressing against her back.

Her head turns, her profile sheer temptation. "I thought you'd forgotten about that."

"Not for a second," I murmur before claiming her lips from behind.

I need her alone. The words were like breaking through a dam. I can't settle for telling her I love her. I want to show her. To prove it with every touch.

I press her against the window until she melts again.

"That first night, I knew you were different," I murmur as I kiss a path down her throat, taking my time.

"Only because I called you on your bullshit. You didn't know what to do with me."

I spin and lift her, her skirt riding up as her legs hook around my hips. I'm used to lifting hundreds of pounds, and she's nothing by comparison.

Nova grips my shoulders. Her body is sweet and soft, and I'm hard and hungry.

I set her down long enough to yank off her skirt. "I want you in my jersey and nothing else."

Her pale skin shines in the moonlight, the curve of her breasts and swell of her hips making my throat dry with longing. I can't see the freckles that dust her shoulders, but I trace them from memory.

I step back to her, my hands skimming up her sides. She sighs against my mouth.

Tonight, I'm going to take my time.

"Get the ice bucket."

I wait for her to bring it over and open the lid.

Surprise flares in her eyes, coupled with curiosity. "What are you going to do?"

"You've been playing a basketball groupie the last few months. Let's see if you've paid attention. Now, lift the jersey as high as it'll go."

She uses both hands to hold the shirt up under her arms.

I take the round ice cube, the large kind like you'd use in scotch, and rub it across the hardened tips of her breasts. "It's all about assembling the right offense to get past the defense."

When she shivers, her thighs clenching, I do it again.

I'm enthralled by the way her body pulls tight. She doesn't hide from me, just watches me through lowered lashes.

"You haven't scored enough this year?" she protests when I move it to the other nipple.

"Not even close."

Nova's low moan is muffled by her lip caught between her teeth. The melting ice trails down the curve of her breast in a tiny river.

"Spread your legs."

She does it without being asked twice.

"Your backcourt handles the ball. Brings it up the court. Takes care of it." I bend my mouth to skin, licking the underside of her breast.

She hiccups.

I trace the melting ice along the bone of her hip. "Gotta protect it so you get it where you need."

Across her stomach.

"Get into the paint, where you can make something happen. The other team's trying to stop you, but you know the secret to being a great shooter?"

Down the inside of her thigh.

"Clay..." Her hips arch toward me.

"Understanding the ball wants to go in the net." I want to take her, to make her mine every way there is. "Spread yourself for me."

She starts to move her feet, and I shake my head. Her fingers slide down her body, and she holds herself apart.

I take a long inhale. She smells like heaven. Warm and ripe and mine, her pussy glistens in the low light from the bedside lamp. I run the ice cube down her pink, waiting slit.

"Ohhhhhh," she whispers, her head falling back and eyes closing.

She's so open with me, so willing. It's the best damn gift, and she doesn't even know it.

"It's your turn next," she whispers.

"If you ice my cock, sweetheart, you're going to be finishing this yourself."

She laughs softly. "Vengeance might be more satisfying."

I grin. "I doubt it."

She's dripping, from the ice cube and her own arousal, her hips arching with every stroke.

I'll give her more, but it won't be what she wants.

I press the ice inside her pussy. Nova gasps when it's high enough her clenching walls hold it there. Her hand skims up her ribcage and absently plays with her breast.

Fuck. I want to tease her all night, but it's too much for a man to handle.

I was planning to wait for the ice to melt, but I'm losing patience. I retrieve it with my fingers and toss it at the trash.

Three points. I say it in my head.

"Two points," she says as if she heard me.

"No way."

"You lose a point for being an asshole."

But on her face, there's only teasing and genuine affection.

I'm going to fuck this girl so hard.

"What?" she asks, smiling.

"Just thinking of all the ways I'm going make you beg."

My lips brush hers, and we catch fire. She tries to help get my clothes off, but I do most of the work because of my height.

"That what you dream about?" she teases.

My pants get caught around my ankle. I'm seconds away from ripping them off, except that'd probably make my knee worse.

"Nah. In my dreams, we're..." I trail off, and she waits.

I glance at my wallet, then take a breath and rock back. "In my dreams, I'm inside you with nothing between us."

We've talked before about how I'm clean and neither of us has slept with anyone else since we started this. I haven't told her I can't imagine fucking anyone else again.

She inhales, and it's the longest moment before she answers. "I dream about that too."

NOVA

I'm here, in Clay's room at the all-star game, wearing only a jersey that's doing nothing to clothe me except for maybe my shoulders. My own personal pro-athlete fantasy is driving me wild with his touch and the ice from the bucket.

But when he hears my answer, he looks... humble.

He loves me. It's plain on every inch of his face, the reverence of his hands.

Clay lifts me, wrapping my legs around his hips and walking me over to the glass doors. The jersey slips down over my breasts, but he doesn't complain.

"You want everyone to see us?" I tease.

"If it means they know I'm the luckiest man in the world because I get to do this to you, with you, then yeah."

My heart skips.

He's huge and hard between us as he positions himself between my thighs.

Clay never gets easier to take, but I get used to him.

I start to ask if he wants me to take the jersey off but think better of it. I like wearing his number like this. I like being his.

When he presses against me where I'm already wet, sinking inside an inch at a time, my head falls back to hit the glass.

"Yeah, sweetheart."

He moves deeper inside me, holding my hips to keep the depth from being too intense.

It's intense anyway.

"Fuck, you feel so good. Too good. Every inch of you hot and wet, squeezing me."

His fingers dig into my ass, and I sigh, an exhale that has me sliding all the way down his cock.

"Clay!"

His grin is apologetic, and I couldn't love him any more.

"Want to be on top?"

I shake my head. "No."

He turns ravenous in a heartbeat.

One hand grabs both of mine, pinning them over my head while he holds me up with his other arm.

Clay starts to pump in and out of me, long, slow strokes that leave me aching and breathless.

When he strokes in, I'm so tight, too tight. But the second he's gone, all I want is for him to fill me again.

Is that what love is? Not comfort and predictability, but throbbing on the edge of freefall?

My hips start to rise to meet his.

He crushes his mouth to mine, lifting me higher so our faces line up.

"You close?" he asks.

"Yes," I pant against his lips.

"Want to hear you scream."

"The entire floor will hear."

"Then make it extra loud. For Miles."

I laugh, and he grins as if I've given him the best gift in the world.

I slip a hand between us, playing with my clit. He takes my breast in his hand, twisting my nipple.

I can't hold on.

Pleasure splits me, and a low moan erupts from my throat. His name follows, and he fists my hair and drags my mouth to his, swallowing my sounds as he thrust into me, fast and furious.

Then he's coming too, a wrenching release that rips through his hard body.

CLAY

It's late when we make it to the bed.

First time is against the windows.

The second is on the chair in the corner.

The third is somewhere between the minifridge and the floor.

I carry her to the king-sized mattress, tugging down the bedspread to lay her between the sheets.

I shift over her, concerned. "You okay?"

I tip her chin toward me so I can look in her eyes.

They crinkle at the corners. "If I didn't already have your jersey, I'd have to buy it."

I chuckle, a feeling that reaches my toes. "Every road game, I want pictures of you in it. No panties. Just like this."

"If I'm naked except for the jersey, I might be too distracted to take pictures."

She nestles against my shoulder, and I twist a piece of her hair around my finger. It's pink against the black ink of my tattoos.

I like this.

I could get used to it.

My heart rate's barely returned to normal when I hear myself speak. "Move in with me."

She pulls back. "What?"

Hell, maybe I have lost my head. But I plow on anyway. "I like waking up and seeing you in my bed. Going to sleep with you next to me."

"We do that already."

It's not the response I hoped for. "But right now, we have to fight for time together. This way, you'd have more than a toothbrush at my place." My life is routines and schedules, and I don't want to leave being with her to chance. "My place won't just be a place you crash but a place you're at home."

The last girl I tried to commit to bailed on me,

and that hurt sneaks up in my chest, a suspicious snake ready to lash out.

"Can I think about it?"

"Yeah." I inch away, but she pulls me back with surprising strength.

"Hey, I didn't say no. I said I want to think about it. I finally feel like I'm getting my life in order, and you've been a big part of that." Her lips brush my ear. Her soft scent fills my nostrils and calms my system. "Would there be space for me to work? There's this show in New York, and... I don't want to get paint in your sports memorabilia room."

The knot of tension between my shoulders eases. "I'll move it out."

I'd build her a thousand studios if she wanted. Let her drag a wet brush across every jersey and game ball.

The moment before I fall asleep, her heart is still thudding against mine, her arms wrapped around me.

I hope to hell that's enough for her.

24

CLAY

They say the all-star game is a perk, not a competition.

But life is a competition.

I'm playing with the best in the league. It's a chance to test myself against every talented, hardworking, genetically blessed guy who ever picked up a basketball and dreamed he could make this his life.

That's the real fun of the entire weekend.

Now, in the huddle around me, there are four other guys representing the best of the Western Conference. Including Kyle Banks, one of LA's stars.

"Hey, Wade. This is gonna be fun to be on the same side for once."

He's not wrong.

We head onto the court and let loose.

The first play up the court, Kyle takes it and tosses an alley-oop to our point forward. On the way back, the East puts on their show with a pump fake chased by a fadeaway.

This is like the Oscars. A celebration of the sport and what we all can do.

The next trip up, I do my part, weaving and dodging before I put it down with a thunderous dunk drowned out by hollering and applause.

Normally, we sub out every few minutes, so when our coach for the night nods at me to sit in exchange for another player, it's performative and not personal.

"Rumor says we might be playing together sooner than later." The voice has me looking over to see Kyle grinning from down the bench. "Need someone ruthless in my camp."

There's respect between us, but he's never been my favorite person. His game has an extra edge mine doesn't. If he can't win straight, he'll win dirty.

Still, I meet his fist with my own before shifting back in my seat to wipe the sweat from my face and enjoy the view. But when I look over, it's Nova in the stands that makes my chest tighten.

She's wearing my jersey and watching the game intensely.

When our eyes meet, she smiles and mouths, "Hey."

"Hey." I beam back at her, feeling giddy like a schoolkid.

Last night, Nova said she loved me.

She let me drag her into my room.

And each touch of her skin, every breathy moan from her lips, the taste of her sweetness when she came in my mouth, and the feel of her squeezing my cock was damned near perfect.

I wish she'd said yes to me asking her to move in, but I get that it's a big deal. I'm trying to be patient and not take it as rejection.

The game carries on, and every few minutes, I sneak glances at her. Each time, she's still there, watching me just like before.

My heart thuds harder. I didn't think this moment could feel better, but she's it—the missing piece.

I want her in my life. I need to convince her she matters as much as basketball, and it's not as simple as moving my trophies to make room for her art.

"Wade, you're up!"

We go back and forth for the next couple of hours.

Ten sweaty pros playing like kids, laughing and grinning and showing off.

The money and the calculations fall away, and it's just love of the game. Ours and everyone else's in this building.

The West wins by five. The charities for both teams get huge donations, so everyone wins.

Still, we get a trophy. Media flocks to do interviews. A bunch of players and ex-players descend, and after I speak to a couple of outlets, a rumbling voice accompanies an arm around my shoulders.

"That knee feel as good as it looks?"

I glance up to see Zane Carter, a Hall of Fame player, watching inquisitively.

"It's better."

I hold out a hand, and he grabs it. I'm still in my jersey, and he's in a designer suit custom fitted to his six-six frame.

"Hell of a game, even for one of these," Zane says.

"Appreciate it."

The guy is a legend in the truest sense. I had his basketball card as a kid. His poster was on my wall.

I catch sight of Nova behind him and can't help smiling.

He follows my gaze. "I hope you make better choices than I did. I got a lot of rings. Only one I couldn't hang onto."

I don't much follow guys' relationships, but the tabloids made a big deal of a couple of his divorces.

"You always reminded me of me," he says.

"That's a high compliment."

"It's a good thing for basketball and a bad thing for you. See, you're relentless. Never see anything outside the court. By the time I looked up, it was too late. I came over because I was relieved to see it doesn't look like that's the way things are anymore for you. Kept seeing how you looked up at the stands, like you're head over heels. Don't lose that."

Another group of guys comes over to congratulate me, but I'm focused on Zane's words.

I can't lose her. I won't.

25

CLAY

"*H*elluva game," Harlan greets me as I drop into the booth opposite him and unzip my jacket. I grab a fry off his plate.

The waitress comes by. "Can I get you something, Clay?"

"Coke. Thanks."

"Rebel." Harlan's eyes crinkle as she departs. "When I came through, you showed up to practice on time and drilled your shots. You were fine. Now everything is about optimizing. Nutrition, sleep—it all gets tracked and improved to the finest point. There's no such thing as good enough."

I turn that over as my Coke arrives and I take a sip. "You sound like you miss those days."

"I miss when guys were treated like people instead of scorecards."

The leather booth creaks as I shift back and study our GM.

He turns his beer in his hand before taking a long sip. "Things are challenging with Coach out. Emotionally, for everyone, because no one figured he'd still be in this position a week out, but also for making decisions. Because deals have to get signed and players need to be locked down. That's why I want to talk about LA."

A bit of the friendliness fades from his eyes, replaced by resoluteness. "I called your manager this weekend—"

"I don't want a trade."

His nostrils flare.

I'm sure the words sound as strange in his ears as they feel in my mouth.

"Since when?"

"A while," I say.

I've always thought taking control of my destiny was about getting to the best team and creating a legacy for myself.

What if I've been seeing it wrong the whole time?

Harlan curses under his breath. "Your entire

career, you've known you were the best. But I won't build a team around a man who doesn't want to be here. Can't put a house on an unwilling foundation."

"I can lead this team," I say.

"But do you want to? Or is this about Nova?"

My hands fist. "I think you're beyond asking questions about my love life. But I wouldn't be the first player to make a decision to stay near the people he cares about."

This is how I'll show her I'm committed to us. To a future together.

I can give her some of the stability she craves without making decisions for her.

Harlan's expression softens a bit. "She's certainly making an impression around here. And I'm sorry for trying to keep you apart. I thought it was for the best, but that doesn't make it right."

I shift in my seat, take another sip of my drink. Guess some part of me thought that too, or I wouldn't have done it. "You still sleeping on the couch?"

"Spare bedroom," he corrects.

"Not much difference."

"Not in the ways that count." Harlan slings an arm over the back of the booth. "Mar's been going through something. But she hasn't talked to me about it."

The fact that he's suffering too blunts my animosity towards him. In this, at least, we're the same.

"I meant what I said, Harlan. I'm committed to this place. This team."

The waitress comes back to offer Harlan another beer, which he declines and then asks for the bill. I nod that I'll pick it up.

"Why'd you want to meet at Mile High?" Harlan asks.

"I haven't been around in a while and wanted to check in."

"Because you like the fries."

I study him, wondering what his game is.

Nova would show her cards and trust that the rest would work itself out.

"Because I own forty-nine percent of this bar."

Harlan stares me down for a minute before he shifts out of his seat and wraps his scarf around his neck, tucking it into his wool coat. "You're full of surprises."

I rise too and reach for my coat. "Thank fuck. I'd hate to be predictable."

He considers, then nods. "LA will be

disappointed to hear they won't be getting a veteran all-star for their post-season lineup. I'll talk to James and confirm with you."

The tension in me releases.

Another week and the trade talk will be dead. Nova will know I'm here for the long haul.

"You realize this is called all-star *break* for a reason?" Jay comments from across the court as he passes to Rookie in practice.

Normally, most of the guys who weren't invited to the all-star game would spend a few days relaxing with friends and family afterward.

Today, I called in a favor and grabbed us the college gym.

"You know who lays on a beach in February? Retirees," I reply.

Rookie grunts as he cuts through the defenders and goes in for the dunk. Atlas stops him, sending him to the floor. Rookie falls on his back, and I'm over the court, extending a hand.

"Layup," he says as he grabs it, shaking his head because he doubts his decision.

"No. You had it. That was a blocking foul." I ignore Atlas's protest. "Take it."

Rookie nods. I pull him up and clap him on the shoulder.

The entire team was supposed to be back for the gala, but I asked them to come a day early to practice. In fact, this is an unscheduled practice. We're at this gym because I don't want anyone knowing what we're doing. None of the coaching staff is here. Only the players. It's off the books. I want a man-to-man talk with the roster.

"Let's keep it going. I gotta be home in an hour," I say.

"Your girl waiting on you with spread... arms?" Atlas amends at my look.

"Nah, I'm moving my trophies and shit out so Nova can move in."

Miles shakes his head. "Still think she'll wake up and realize her mistake."

"It's not a mistake. She's mine and I'm hers."

They all stare at me.

"Now get back to work."

We finish running the drills. I jump in to get the reps and prove I'm not only good for talking.

After, I gather the team around a whiteboard.

"Next week, we're going to LA. Back-to-back. One guess what our goal is."

"Get Kim Kardashian to sign my dick?" Rookie volunteers.

I grab a marker.

"Wow, he's really lost his mind," Atlas mutters to Jayden.

I write four numbers on the board, a hyphen separating the first two and second two. "You know what this is?"

"Our record."

I write another number. Three. "What about this?"

This time there's hesitation.

"Games out," Rookie says.

"That's the number of games out of first place we are."

One more number.

"How many teams are ahead of us. And this is the bonus round." I write one final number. *Ten.*

Jay frowns. "It's not the number of games we need to get a playoff spot."

"That's the number of games we need to win to guarantee home court for the first series."

"Home court." Atlas laughs. "We've never had home court."

"Otherwise, we play somewhere like this. Unfamiliar. Hostile. I want our fans in the seats. Our banners in the rafters. Our colors on the floor. Not because we can't beat a team on the road. Because when we do this, I want witnesses."

The guys exchange looks.

"We can win ten games," Rookie says, but it's cockiness, not belief.

"You tell me." I look at him.

Rookie knows what I'm asking. "Yeah. We can."

I turn to Miles.

"Sure, Clay."

Atlas. This guy's been around a few teams, made deep playoff runs.

He nods.

Then Jayden. My long-time friend and teammate.

"What do you say, Jay? We gonna take ten?"

He frowns. "Let's take 'em all."

A cheer goes up.

After we finish, Jay waits a bit for the room to empty, grabbing for his towel on the seats. "What was that about? Not that I don't appreciate the *Mighty Ducks* shit, but it's not your style."

"Maybe my style is changing." I drag off my

practice jersey and stuff it into my bag, reaching for a fresh T-shirt.

He checks his phone. "Hear LA is looking to make some trades. Deadline is the day of the gala."

"Won't be with me."

Jay's eyes narrow. "How do you know?"

"Because I asked Harlan not to. And he owes me."

My friend's tense face dissolves into disbelief. "You're staying?"

Harlan's commitment replays in my mind.

"I'm staying."

He grabs me in a hug so hard it's my turn to be stunned. It didn't occur to me that this was eating him up so much. But I can feel his relief and happiness.

Come to think of it, I'm pretty glad to be staying too.

26

NOVA

"You look incredible," Brooke says as she stands behind me in the mirror.

I turn sideways, smoothing my hands down the silver dress.

I'm picking out an outfit for the gala Saturday night. Nearly a thousand people are attending, from billionaires to politicians to executives and every important person from the team's history.

I can't wait for the big reveal of the mural.

After the all-star game, seeing the guys laugh and cheer and play jokes on one another, I knew exactly what I needed to finish my artwork.

The third element was unexpected, but it's actually perfect.

I hope everyone loves it as much as I do.

"It's your night," Brooke goes on.

"It's the team's night."

"But it's your coming-out party."

A happy flush rises up my cheeks as I show her the picture Clay took earlier of me in front of the finished installation.

"It's stunning, Nova."

"Chloe's sending me the program soon. I get to introduce it. That's partly why I need this dress."

I turn in the outfit, then check the price tag.

Grumpy Baller: Send me a picture.

I do.

He texts back a picture of his credit card.

Grumpy Baller: No protests.

I bite my cheek.

I let him buy the dress, but I spot another one on a rack and lift it off. "I want this one too. But put it on my card."

The plastic clicks on the counter as I set my card in front of the cashier. It feels good to have my own money to pay for things.

"Can I have it delivered? And could I include a message?"

"Of course." She passes over a card and pen.

"Who's that for?" Brooke asks.

I scrunch my brows together, my bare toes gripping the soft carpet as I write out a note to be enclosed in the box. "My sister."

"Nova. You getting dressed?" Clay calls from the living room of his place.

"Almost ready," I reply through the bathroom door, checking my phone and cursing.

Brooke insisted we have someone do our hair for the gala, but I fiddled with my makeup way too long before changing.

We're almost late. The program starts in an hour. Plus, we said we'd meet Brooke and her date there early.

One last look in the mirror. My pink shoes give me an extra four inches of height. The pink gloss makes my lips shine, but the subtle smoky eye feels grown-up.

I'm me, but a grown-up, confident version.

I open the door and head down the hallway,

careful not to trip in the shoes. At the other end, Clay is in a tux, and my breath catches.

It's the first I've seen him like that since the wedding, and I forgot how handsome he looks. Not only sexy, but a dark knight, tattoos snaking out of his cuffs and collar.

He turns, and his expression tightens. "Jesus."

"You like it?" I strike a pose, one hand on my hip as I try to be casual.

This moment is overwhelming.

It's both of our nights.

The trade deadline is looming, and I haven't wanted to ask because I don't want to know the answer.

He crosses to me, and the intensity on his face is unlike anything I've ever seen. Clay stops a few inches away, forcing my chin up so I can meet his half-lidded eyes.

"I like the dress," he murmurs, his gaze running slowly over my curves. "I like the hair." His lips twist. "I fucking love you." He huffs out a breath. "From the moment I met you. And I want to show you something."

He walks me to the closed door of the second bedroom, pushing it wide.

The sports memorabilia is gone.

Instead, there's a stack of easels in one corner. Open shelving that houses canvases and papers. A table lined with every kind of paint and drawing tool imaginable.

"What is this?" I ask, awestruck.

"It's yours. I'm staying with the Kodiaks. Harlan and I worked it out. Tonight, it'll be official."

I grab his bowtie and pull him down to me. His lips claim mine as he wraps his muscled arms around my waist, scooping me up.

I know how much going to LA meant to him, which is why I'm overwhelmed that he decided to do this.

"You're unbelievable," I whisper against his lips.

My phone and his explode at the same time.

Brooke: WHERE THE HELL ARE YOU?!

Shit.

Clay reluctantly sets me down, and I swipe at the corner of my lips to try to stop my lipstick from smudging more.

"We'll pick this up."

We sure as hell will.

On the walk to the car, we're hand in hand, and I'm practically floating.

I try to refocus during the drive, reminding myself of what's happening tonight. It's my crowning achievement.

When we get to the stadium, I reach for my ID, but security waves us in the back way.

As we approach the party, I see the wall is covered in draperies in the team's colors.

"Where's your date?" I ask Brooke when we find her.

"He bailed." Her smile is tight. "It's fine."

"I'll get you a drink," Clay offers.

"Make it two," Brooke calls.

I spot Miles halfway across the room, and I motion him over, pulling him down to my ear when he gets close enough. "Brooke's date stood her up. Do with that what you will."

He's immediately on alert.

The program starts, and James goes to the front. "Sports are eternal. They're about what we can achieve that's never been done before. Now, I recognize there's a damper over the evening because of our former coach's absence. But the Kodiaks are celebrating the past, and more than that, we're celebrating the future.

"Tonight marks a turning point in this team's future. A changing of the guard, so to speak. We are burning the ashes of our past to rise anew."

He motions to someone in the corner, and the curtain drops.

A collective gasp goes up. My heart pounds at the response.

My wall is beautiful.

Applause starts, hollers jumping in.

"Nova! Nova! Nova!"

Miles starts the chant, the other guys joining until there's a chorus of voices. Clay nods, a secret smile meant only for me. Tears form behind my eyes.

Clay calls, "Take a bow, Pink."

I go to the front and step in front of the owner.

"I'm so glad you all like it. I appreciate the opportunity to get to know the team. The buildings represent the city. The faces are the team. And the bears are family. Because this is a family."

My gaze locks with familiar eyes in the back.

Mari.

As soon as I finish my speech, I race across the room to my sister and throw my arms around her. "You came!"

"I couldn't not be here on my baby sister's big day." Her smile is tentative at first. "You said it— family is everything." Her hand rests on her stomach. Stays there.

I gasp. "Mari. Are you pregnant?!"

She nods. "Two months. I was having some hormone problems, and that was contributing to my emotional swings. I've never felt so out of control, and someone from the office went on maternity leave and got fired, so I was a little stressed over it all. Then when I found out about you and Clay, I overreacted. I'm sorry. I guess it's hard to break the habit of worrying over you."

"Well, now you have someone else to worry about." I nod to her stomach.

"Is it selfish to say I hope you'll stick around Denver? You can be part of the baby's life."

"I'd love that."

She throws her arms around me, and I hug her back every bit as hard.

"Where is Harlan?" I ask.

"He's been busy working all day on the trade deadline. Even when there's not a big deal, he's on the phones until the bitter end, and—there he is!"

Harlan appears from nowhere, his tie hanging around his neck and his eyes weary.

"Nova, I tried. I'm sorry." His expression is pained. "Tell Clay I'm sorry. There was nothing I could do."

"What are you...?" I shake my head. He does owe me an apology for all the mess he caused, but this seems overly heartfelt for him.

When I go to find Clay, he's surrounded by teammates and grinning.

"Can you keep a secret?" I murmur.

"Anything for you."

"Mari is pregnant. I'm going to be an aunt." I'm bubbling over with excitement.

"That's good news," he says.

"The best news," I say tearfully without being able to explain why. I always felt as though we were short-changed in the family department and like me putting my dreams first cost me family.

Now, I can have both things.

A murmur goes up.

"What the fuck?" Miles demands, looking at his phone.

"Nova..." Brooke runs up to me.

Clay pulls out his phone. Whatever he sees, his happiness is gone in an instant.

My heart hammers as I pull his phone toward me.

It's a news article.

It's not true.

When I look up, Harlan's standing next to the owner, looking grim.

It is true.

Clay's jaw locks, his beautiful eyes full of torment.

I look back down at the screen, my chest tightening until I can't breathe.

TRADE RUMOR CONFIRMED:
Denver Kodiaks Forward Clayton Wade Sent to LA in Multiyear Deal for Kyle Banks

Thank you for reading Game Changer! I hope you loved Clay and Nova's emotional, sexy romance.

Their story concludes in Play Maker (coming

August 2023), available to pre-order now at major bookstores.

xoxo,

Piper

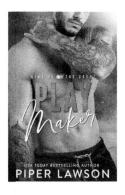

I had everything.
The girl. The team. The dream.
Until in one cruel twist, it all came tumbling down.
I've hit rock bottom with no one to blame but myself.
One last chance is all I'll get.
No one works harder than me—on or off the court.
I will take my team to the next level.
I will make the woman I love mine for good.
One last play for everything I've wanted my entire life.

Order Play Maker now!

For writing updates, early excerpts and exclusive giveaways...

Join my VIP List and never miss a thing!

www.piperlawsonbooks.com/subscribe

KING OF THE COURT SERIES

After being dumped and losing my job the same week, the last thing my broken heart needs is a rebound.

A steamy, grumpy sunshine sports romance featuring a woman down on her luck, a star basketball player with a filthy mouth, and a connection neither of them can deny.

OFF-LIMITS SERIES

Turns out the beautiful man from the club is my new professor... But he wasn't when he kissed me.

Off-Limits is a forbidden age gap college romance series. Find out what happens when the beautiful man from the club is Olivia's hot new professor.

WICKED SERIES

Rockstars don't chase college students. But Jax Jamieson never followed the rules.

Wicked is a new adult rock star series full of nerdy girls, hot rock stars, pet skunks, and ensemble casts you'll want to be friends with forever.

RIVALS SERIES

At seventeen, I offered Tyler Adams my home, my life, my heart. He stole them all.

Rivals is an angsty new adult series. Fans of forbidden romance, enemies to lovers, friends to lovers, and rock star romance will love these books.

ENEMIES SERIES

I sold my soul to a man I hate. Now, he owns me.

Enemies is an enthralling, explosive romance about an American DJ and a British billionaire. If you like wealthy, royal alpha males, enemies to lovers, travel or sexy romance, this series is for you!

TRAVESTY SERIES

My best friend's brother grew up. Hot.

Travesty is a steamy romance series following best friends who start a fashion label from NYC to LA. It contains best friends brother, second chances, enemies to lovers, opposites attract and friends to lovers stories. If you like sexy, sassy romances, you'll love this series.

PLAY SERIES

I know what I want. It's not Max Donovan. To hell with his money, his gaming empire, and his joystick.

Play is an addictive series of standalone romances with slow burn tension, delicious banter, office romance and unforgettable characters. If you like smart, quirky, steamy enemies-to-lovers, contemporary romance, you'll love Play.

MODERN ROMANCE SERIES

When your rich, handsome best friend asks you to be his fake girlfriend? Say no.

Modern Romance is a smart, sexy series of contemporary romances following a set of female friends running a relationship marketing company in NYC. If you enjoy hot guys who treat their families like gold, fun antics, dirty talk, real characters, steamy scenes, badass heroines and smart banter, you'll love the Modern Romance series.

ABOUT THE AUTHOR

Piper Lawson is a WSJ and USA Today bestselling author of smart and steamy romance.

She writes women who follow their dreams, best friends who know your dirty secrets and love you anyway, and complex heroes you'll fall hard for.

Piper lives in Canada with her tall and brilliant husband. She's a sucker for dark eyes, dark coffee, and dark chocolate.

For a complete reading list, visit
www.piperlawsonbooks.com/books

**Subscribe to Piper's VIP email list
www.piperlawsonbooks.com/subscribe**

amazon.com/author/piperlawson

bookbub.com/authors/piper-lawson

instagram.com/piperlawsonbooks

facebook.com/piperlawsonbooks

goodreads.com/piperlawson

ACKNOWLEDGMENTS

When I started writing Clay and Nova's story, I imagined it being wrapped up in a single book. Looking back, there's no way that would have done them justice.

I loved having the space and breathing room to sink deeper into their relationship and to inhabit their world, and I hope you enjoy it as much as I do.

Shot Taker wouldn't have happened without the support of my awesome readers, including my ARC team. You ladies provide endless enthusiasm, cheerleading, and help spreading the word. Thank you.

Becca Mysoor: Thank you for making me believe that everything is possible and leading by example. I treasure our friendship more than I can say.

Cassie Robertson: Thank you for bringing consistency to my wacky ideas, and for laughing at my jokes in the margins (but only the good ones).

Devon Burke: Thank you for helping polish my stories into their best selves, and for bringing your incredible heart and wisdom to the task.

Annette Brignac and Kate Tilton: Thank you for being in my corner, for seeing what I'm trying to create in the world and creating it with me. Without you, few things would get done and probably none of it would get done well.

Lori Jackson and Emily Wittig: Thank you for taking my random ideas and wacky gradients and making art from them. I'm grateful you still respond to my emails.

Nina Grinstead and the entire VPR team: thank you for your wisdom, support, and tireless effort to help readers find books they'll love.

Last but not least, thank YOU for reading. Truly. Knowing we're living in these words and worlds together is the best part of any gig I've ever had.

Love always,

Piper

ONE MORE THING

As I write this—the notes page, not the book, which I finished weeks ago—Denver's IRL pro basketball team is celebrating a newly minted championship after beating Miami last night.

It's their first ever.

Obviously, I can't take credit for this achievement.

All I can say is that I've been sending them good vibes for months now.

Readers, you know I love bringing you as much accuracy as possible when I dive into a new world! And since basketball is one of my fave sports, I've sprinkled in as many real challenges, situations, and terms as possible.

My hardcore basketball fans might notice that the trade deadline takes place immediately after the all-star game in this story.

IRL at the time of writing, the two are reversed. But it worked better for the story to have them this way, so I hope you'll forgive me.

(And fun fact: until 2017, they did occur this way until league commissioner switched them. So by the time you're reading this, maybe they'll be swapped back ;))

Printed in Great Britain
by Amazon

24038158R00172